Harry Cook

Felix
Silver,
Teaspoons &
Witches

duet

interlude **press**

CHICAGO

Copyright © 2022 by Harry Cook
All rights reserved
Published by Duet of Interlude Press
An imprint of Chicago Review Press Incorporated
814 North Franklin Street
Chicago, Illinois 60610
ISBN 978-1-951954-14-7

Library of Congress Cataloging-in-Publication Data
Names: Cook, Harry, 1991– author.
Title: Felix Silver, teaspoons & witches / Harry Cook.
Other titles: Felix Silver, teaspoons and witches
Description: Chicago, Illinois : Duet of Interlude Press, [2022] |
    Audience: Ages 12 & up. | Summary: Felix and his new friends, including
    his crush Aero, turn to Felix's Grandma Aggie and the witches of Dorset
    Harbor to help them find a group of missing teenagers and combat the
    dark magic that is creeping into town.
Identifiers: LCCN 2022016810 | ISBN 9781951954147 (trade paperback) | ISBN
    9781951954154 (ebook)
Subjects: CYAC: Magic—Fiction. | Witches—Fiction. | Missing
    persons—Fiction. | LGBTQ+ people—Fiction. | Fantasy. | BISAC: YOUNG
    ADULT FICTION / LGBTQ+ | YOUNG ADULT FICTION / Fantasy / Wizards &
    Witches | LCGFT: Fantasy fiction.
Classification: LCC PZ7.1.C64739 Fe 2022 | DDC [Fic]—dc23
LC record available at https://lccn.loc.gov/2022016810

Cover and interior design: CB Messer

Printed in the United States of America

For my family, who allowed me to believe in magic

NO LONGER PROPERTY OF
SEATTLE PUBLIC LIBRARY

NO LONGER PROPERTY OF
SEATTLE PUBLIC LIBRARY

"I address you all tonight for who you truly are: wizards, mermaids, travelers, adventurers, and magicians. You are the true dreamers."

—Brian Selznick, *The Invention of Hugo Cabret*

Part One

Alone

One

"You know your father and I love you, right?" Mum says as she puts the car in park and pulls the hand brake.

I nod. This is awkward. Ever since Mum and Dad announced their divorce, they've been tiptoeing around me like I may have a full-blown meltdown.

"It's… You're such a special boy, Felix."

Here we go. Insert eye roll.

So apparently, I have these powers. Just weird circumstances that appear to point in the direction that I'm one of the "gifted ones," like Grandma Aggie. It started with minor stuff: acing some exams without studying or my room miraculously becoming spotless after I forgot to tidy up like Dad had asked me to.

Nothing seemed too off until the afternoon, when I found myself hovering above a rusty old nail on the stairwell to our basement. Firstly, thank fuck. Secondly, what!? Levitating? I quickly dropped down to the step below and steadied myself for a moment while trying to realize what had happened. It's tricky to deny something weird is going on when you lift off the ground like a hummingbird.

Mum has always been pretty quiet when it comes to her own abilities. I remember catching her using the occasional charm when I was much younger, but ever since her and Dad started fighting, I haven't seen a flicker of it.

So here we are, five hours from our house in Oakington. They think it wise that I live here in Dorset Harbor to learn from Grandma Aggie while they sort out their Jerry Springer divorce proceedings. To be honest, I'm kind of looking forward to a change of scenery.

Mum unclips her seatbelt and stares up at the house for a moment, leaving the car running so the only sound is the whirr of the air conditioning. It's 10:39 PM, and the only light nearby comes from the big bay windows nestled within the climbing ivy curled around them.

The wraparound porch with white trim houses the giant oak front door while the chimney to the side of the house puffs little marshmallow clouds of smoke like a steam train.

"Are you OK?" I ask, fiddling with a thread of cotton from my ripped blue jeans.

Now it's Mum's turn to nod. "Ready?"

She grabs her handbag from the back seat, squeezes my hand, and turns off the ignition.

The air is chilly as we get out of the car, the only sounds coming from the creaking branches of the oak tree and the distant waves lapping up against the wharf from the harbor nearby.

"I know it's been a while since you last saw Nan Aggie," Mum says as we ascend the porch stairs. "And as much as she means well, she can be a bit—"

"A bit what, darling?" Grandma Aggie says from the doorway, letting the light from inside pool around our feet.

She is exactly as I remember her. A top knot bun of wild strawberry-blonde curls sit atop her head. Her dress is polka dot, her corset a deep purple velvet. Each finger is embellished with a different gemstone ring, and her boots are black leather with a silver and gold buckle.

"Hey," Mum says, leaning in for a hug. "I was going to say eccentric."

"Ha! I prefer potty, bonkers, or batsh—"

"Don't," Mum says with a look of fierce disapproval.

Grandma Aggie giggles before licking her thumb and rubbing a lipstick mark from Mum's cheek.

"Felix, as I live and breathe," she says, pulling me in for a hug.

I'm instantly hit by her signature smell: cocoa, Estée Lauder Youth-Dew perfume, and dust.

"I've missed you, my little spud. Gosh, I've missed you." She pulls me in closer. "Come, come. I've made a fresh pot of tea."

We head inside, where I put my bags by the stairwell, then head into the dining room and find a seat around her round table. A steaming pot of tea sits in the middle around some teacups, French Fancies, thin pink wafers, and custard creams for dunking.

"Everything in life starts with a good cup of tea," Gran says, pulling up a chair next to me. "How are you doing, Wanda?"

Mum shifts uncomfortably in her chair and stares into her teacup. "Good. I'm, uh… Henry and I both have lawyers now, so that's fun."

"Ooh, joy," Gran says. "I don't mean to say I told you so, especially in front of Spud here, but—"

"OK, well, let's just change the sub—" Mum starts.

"I just mean he's never exactly had your best interests at heart. He's never been very supportive of your… Well, your talents."

The room suddenly feels warm and void of air. Gran gives me a little wink and a smile, and I dunk a custard cream in my tea. I really don't know how to process their split. On the one hand, they're clearly miserable together. On the other, there's still that little bit of hope I'm holding onto. I guess this is another one of the many reasons I don't exactly trust the whole idea of love and a happily ever after.

"You're more than welcome to stay too, you know," Gran says, leaning over to put her hand on Mum's.

"As appealing as that offer is," Mum says, "I'd only distract Felix from his studies."

Gran nods and takes a sip of her tea. "You'll stay for dinner?"

"Sure," Mum says, shrugging off whatever she was feeling a moment before.

Gran rubs her hands together. "Spud, your room is upstairs and to the right. Take your bags up, get comfy, scroll through Instabook or Facegram or whatnot. Your mum and I are going to have some girl talk. Dinner will be ready soon."

I have no idea how dinner will be ready soon, considering it's nearly 11 PM and nothing smells remotely cooked, but I head out into the hall, grab my bag, and head upstairs to my new room.

The house is cozy, to say the least. It's not the typical home you expect your seventy-three-year-old grandma to reside in, I suppose. The walls are lined with paintings and sketches from famous artists, the wallpaper a light, mossy green. An old broom sits in the corner of the landing by my room, and above is a large ornate mirror with gemstones embedded within the frame.

Gran has definitely tried her best to give my room a teenage feel. The movie posters on the walls are not exactly *my* kind of movies—*The Great Train Robbery* and *Gone with The Wind*—but it's still a nice gesture. She's brought in a sound system, a TV, and a small desk in the corner with an old lamp that looks like it belongs in a museum. On it sits a stack of books by authors like Gloria Steinem and Maya Angelou.

I flop down on my bed like a starfish and let myself breathe. Uprooting and starting fresh in Dorset Harbor wasn't really my ideal start to senior year, but I'm excited to spend some time with Grandma Aggie. The last time I visited we had chocolate cake for breakfast, so it's without a doubt going to be more exciting than watching my parents throw verbal grenades at each other across the breakfast table.

The muffled sounds of Mum and Gran downstairs drift up through the floorboards as I clamber off the bed and retrieve my phone from my bag.

As I turn back to my bed, I'm greeted by what I can only describe as two hundred pounds of fur and slobber.

"NEWT!" I shout at the enormous English mastiff that has decided to sit in the center of my bed. "OFF!"

Newt blinks and smashes his tail against the bedsheets, clearly ecstatic to have been found and simultaneously trying to beat my mattress to death.

"How the hell did you get in here?"

He stands on all fours, staring at me with those big dopey eyes, and then he spins around a few times before tackling me to the floor.

Newt has been Gran's dog for as long as I can remember. He will eat just about anything—including me, I'm sure, if I ever decided to sleep in past 10 AM or die.

The dog makes a beeline for my bag and dips his enormous head into the contents of it. He'd be a great sniffer dog at airports if he wasn't the size of a horse.

I'm about to pull his enormous face out of my toiletry bag when three knocks from below rattle me.

"Spud! Dinner in a tick!" Grandma Aggie shouts up through the floorboards.

The word "dinner" sends Newt crashing through the door and down the stairs. I follow slowly, wiping the slobber onto my jeans.

When I arrive back in the dining room, I'm surprised to find Mum and Gran sitting in front of empty plates.

"I, uh, thought you said dinner was—"

"Oh, pshhh," Gran says, giving me a kiss on the cheek. "And *there* you are, my little blossom," she says to Newt, who nearly knocks the crystal from the sideboard with his baseball bat of a tail. Gran glances between me and Mum and adjusts the rose quartz ring on her pinky finger. "Now, what do we feel like?"

"Are we getting takeout?" I ask.

"Takeout? Have you lost your mind?" Gran says, patting Newt's giant head as he sits beside her. "No no no. I'm cooking."

I check the clock. It's nearly 11:30 PM and there's not a pot or pan in sight.

Mum takes a sip of wine. "Something simple is fine."

"Red wine goes well with a roast, no?" Gran says, taking a sip of hers too.

"It's far too late for that."

"Too late for that?" Gran says. "As if my name isn't Agnes Silver."

With that, Gran takes a teaspoon from her corset pocket that looks like nothing I've seen before. Small, silver, with a beautiful emerald in the base and intricate grooves throughout the handle. She taps it three times against her empty teacup as a low hum fills the room.

"Do you have a butler or someth—" Before I can finish my sentence, an enormous crash sounds from the kitchen next to us.

Grandma Aggie raises an eyebrow and then stands, motioning us to follow her.

When we get to the kitchen, it looks like a war zone. The cupboard doors rattle like they're in the eye of a hurricane. The whir of a blender mixed with the clang of pots that whizz by our ears and catapult themselves toward the stove make me duck like we're in the line of fire. A chef's knife hurtles toward a roast chicken that is brown, crispy, and somehow cooked and prepared, as if from a five-star restaurant.

"Mum! I thought we could at least EASE HIM INTO IT!" my mum shouts over the roaring bubble of gravy on the stove.

Grandma Aggie just giggles as she busies herself with some potatoes in a pot.

Within five minutes, we are sitting in front of our plates in the dining room again, each with our own serving of delicious roast chicken, parsnips, potatoes, vegetables, and gravy.

Grandma Aggie has a rogue piece of cauliflower in her hair as she takes a breath and a sip of her wine. She slices into a piece of chicken. "So, Spud, are you ready to learn the Silver way?"

Two

I WAKE TO THE SOUND of Newt snoring next to my bed. I don't remember inviting him in my room last night, but he's made himself comfy by curling half his body into a horse-shaped ball in my suitcase and the other half on the carpet, a puddle of drool around his saggy jowls.

I'm still trying to wrap my head around the events of the last twenty-four hours. I've always known Gran had powers, but to see them in action is a totally different story. On top of that, I've woken up with the usual tight knot in my stomach about Mum and Dad's divorce. It's been on my mind a lot lately, and this morning my anxiety has decided to go into overdrive, go figure. *This* is precisely the reason I have no trust in love. It never ends like it does in the movies.

I go downstairs to find Gran at the kitchen bench, a notepad and pen in front of her and a cup of tea in a saucer next to her. The room seems to have gone back to how it was before the pyrotechnic display of dinner I witnessed last night.

"Darling," Gran says. "What can I get you? Cereal? Toast? Chocolate mud cake?"

"Coffee would be great," I say, pulling up a stool at the bench.

"Coffee it is. So sophisticated." Gran smiles. "You're growing up far too fast."

I'm seventeen. Coffee is a necessity if I'm expected to have a normal conversation at eight o'clock in the morning.

"How did you sleep?" Gran asks.

"Great, thanks."

Newt drunkenly gallops over to Gran, sitting patiently beside her and looking around the room like he's expecting bacon to drop from the ceiling. Then again, I don't blame him after what I saw last night.

"Ohh, you're a good boy," Gran says. I look up, expecting her to be talking to me, but instead, she's kissing Newt on his giant head and rubbing his chin. "Here you go, Spud."

The coffee Gran has been making hovers with her hand movement, drifts over to me in midair, then lands delicately in front of me.

"Milk. Sugar," Gran says, flicking her wrist in my direction like the conductor of a marching band.

I go to find the milk and sugar myself when the fridge and a pantry door open, and both items float over and land on the table next to my mug.

"Th-Thanks," I say.

My mind drifts back to Mum and Dad. Should I message them to check in? My hand fumbles in my pocket for my phone, but I change my mind. Mum told me to focus on my craft. That's what she wants for me.

"I am so glad you're here," Gran says. "I always knew you were my special boy. Right from the get-go." Her bejeweled hand rests on mine and strokes my knuckles. She adjusts a bangle on her wrist. "So, what do you say we head into town so I can show you around?"

"Sounds good."

"I really have missed you, darling." Gran's voice is warmer than a tray of freshly baked cookies.

"I've missed you too."

After a shower, I throw on some jeans, a white tee, and my busted, white Converse and survey myself in the mirror in the hall. I'm no James Dean, but it's my look, I guess. I give my hair a shake and try to tousle it into some sort of styled shape before heading downstairs to find Gran waiting for me, car keys in hand.

"No broomstick?" I say with a chuckle, pointing to the old broom next to the coatrack that's seen better days.

Gran looks at the long oak handle and wheat-like bristles. "Oh, that thing? Haven't flown in years. They expect you to retake your test at seventy, and I strictly refuse."

"I was just kidding," I say, but Gran is already halfway out the door and flitting toward her 1959 apple-green Chevy Impala.

I hop in and look for the seatbelt. "Nice wheels, Gran."

"Thanks, love." Gran turns the ignition. "No seatbelts in this old girl. Made before they were trendy."

The engine putters to life as Gran backs out of the drive.

I have to hand it to Dorset Harbor: this place is cute. Lush, green meadows fly by as we dart down the small laneways passing as roads. All the buildings look old and covered in moss, each spouting a different chimney that puffs milky-white smoke into the morning air.

We turn a corner, and the harbor, in all its glory, comes in to view.

I don't know whether it's because I haven't been here in a while or because I'm getting older, but the town is so beautiful. Little cottages look down from the cliffs at the cerulean water below. A few stray seagulls squawk in unison as we find a parking spot next to a large pub that goes by the name the White Horse.

"Perfect day for a pie, a beer, and a stroll around the farmer's market," Gran says.

"I'm seventeen," I say, concealing a snicker. "And it's eleven o'clock in the morning."

Gran gets out of the car. "Ooh, good point. We'll make it a gin and tonic."

"I, uh… Mum would kill me."

"You're still a worrywart, I see." Gran links her arm through mine and leads me toward the White Horse.

Inside, we find ourselves a table by the back. Gran heads to the bar to buy us god knows what.

When she gets back, she's all smiles as she puts her small leather handbag next to her. "So, tell me everything."

I shake my head. I don't really have much to tell.

"How are you doing with the whole divorce thing? Excited to go to Harbor High?" Gran reaches into her bag and takes out a mint, offering me one, which I take. "Any lovers in your life?"

That makes me scoff. "Nada. Nope. Zero. No love in my life. I think Mum and Dad's divorce is a pretty good repellent for that."

Gran leans over and strokes my hand gently. "Try not to let their stuff interfere."

"I guess I haven't found the right person."

"Person?" Gran looks at me quizzically.

"Guy."

Gran strokes my hand again and smiles like I've just told her that the White Horse is doling out free pie. "I always knew you were special. Love, my darling, is one of the greatest potions of all."

I'm about to change the subject, but thankfully our food is delivered by the burly bearded guy who was behind the bar a moment before.

"Thanks," I say as we start tucking in.

Gran eats faster than me, which is saying something, considering I once won a hot dog eating contest back in Oakington. When she's finished, she dabs her mouth with a napkin and reaches into her bag for her pocket mirror to check out her hair and lipstick.

Gran snaps her pocket mirror shut. "Well, my darling, I'm sure there are plenty of young fellas who'll be vying for your heart when you start school."

I roll my eyes into the back of my head and snort. "I doubt that."

"Doubt away. I have a sense when love is on the horizon, and it sure as shiitake mushrooms isn't me!"

We leave the White Horse, and Gran links her arm in mine again. Although it's a bit chilly out, Gran is warm and soft, her hand occasionally patting mine to point at various shops or roads I need to take note of.

"Now, we need to pick up a few bits from the farmer's market first, and then we'll stop by my shop for afternoon tea. You can meet the rest of the gang." Gran makes a beeline to a large square full of stalls filled with potatoes, vegetables, fresh corn, and knickknacks on display. "Winifred is a dear, but she's not the greatest at customer service, and she's been having some trouble at the shop lately. Her familiar isn't too friendly either."

"Her what?"

"Familiar. Newt. Our animal guardians, pets, and snuggle buddies," Gran says as she heads toward a stall selling roasted chestnuts. "Two bags of your most roasted nuts, please."

"So, why don't I have a familiar?"

"Ohh, you will, you will." Gran hands me a bag of chestnuts which are, simply put, freaking delicious. "Our familiars arrive when we're ready, magically speaking. Newt turned up shortly after I brewed my first potion."

"Right," I start as Gran throws her arms up in excitement.

"Tomkin!"

A short man with furrowed eyebrows, bright red socks sprouting from old boots, and a tweed jacket hugging a stout frame stands before us with half a smile.

"Aggie," he says, his voice a squeaky, Southern drawl. "How y'all feeling on this fine morning?"

"Fab," Gran says. "Just fab. This is Felix, my grandson I was telling you about?"

Tomkin outstretches his hand, which I shake.

"Thistle," he says. "Tomkin Thistle."

"Nice to meet you."

"And you," Tomkin says. "I work at the library, just up there on the hill."

"Cool," I say. "Big book fan."

This small talk is excruciating.

"And this is my darling, Melon," he says, motioning to a small green head poking out from the inside pocket of his tweed.

I jump back, alarmed, and try to hide behind Gran. "Is that a snake?"

"Oh, gosh, no." Tomkin takes Melon out of his pocket and reveals the shell the green head is housed in. "A Mississippi map turtle," he says proudly. "I brought her with me when my family moved back to England."

Melon glances around sleepily. "Cute," I say.

"Cute?" Tomkin furrows his brow again. "Don't let her little face and shell fool ya. One wrong move and she'd snap your damn fingers off and spit out the French tips."

"OK, that's, uh… wow."

"We're just grabbing a few things here and then heading over to the Silver Teacup, if you fancy joining?" Gran says, biting into another chestnut.

"Can't, my darlin', I've got to get back to work," Tomkin says, looking up at the library on the hill. "My granddaughter, Fern, she goes to Harbor High. I'll make sure she keeps an eye on you. Especially what with everything going on."

I nod and smile, without a clue what he's on about.

Gran gives him a kiss on the cheek, and we make our way through the crowded marketplace, Tomkin whispering sweet nothings to Melon as he heads in the opposite direction.

"When did Tomkin move to Dorset Harbor?" I ask Gran.

"Oh, about forty years ago, I'd say. Left for the States when he was a baby and came back when he inherited the family cottage."

"That's an old turtle!" I say.

Gran winks, then turns her attention to her shopping.

After Gran has finished buying various herbs and vegetables, we walk past the peaceful harbor, up a cobblestoned alleyway, and around a corner, finding ourselves outside the Silver Teacup. It's small building with mossy old brickwork and a faded purple awning over the front door. The window houses a cute display of teacups balancing on top of one another and various jars and pots full of tea leaves.

We're about to head into the shop when the door flings open and a plump, short woman with curly gray hair and one of the sweetest smiles I've ever seen stands waiting for us. What is with people around here opening doors before anyone arrives?

"Winifred!" Gran says, beaming.

"At last!" Winifred says, eyeing me up and down and looking between Gran and me. "My goodness, how you've grown!"

I can't help but grin. I don't recall ever meeting Winifred, but she's ridiculously cute.

Once inside, Winifred ushers us over to a few armchairs around a small wooden chest. The Silver Teacup is more like a cozy living room than an actual tea shop. There's carpet, for starters. Thick, fluffy cream carpet that armchairs, tables, and stools sit comfortably upon. The walls are lined with shelves filled with various teas and herbs, and antique lamps cast warm, golden light throughout.

Winifred puts a couple of logs on the small fireplace in the corner of the room before joining us, and then sits comfortably on a faded pink armchair. She pours us each a cup of tea and then takes a sip from her own cup.

"I'm so glad you're here. Rotten customers this morning."

"What happened, Win?" Gran asks, eyeing me with a small smirk in the corner of her lips.

"Oh, you know, just the usual. They ask for peppermint when all we have is chai. They ask if we have change for a fifty when we only have change for a twenty. They ask me to not call their child a thieving little pillock, and apparently I'm the devil incarnate."

"Oh, Win, you didn't," Gran says.

"I most certainly did. I caught the little blighter with his hand jammed in the custard cream tin," Winifred says proudly. "I nearly gave him a clip around the ear."

Gran shakes her head as she takes a sip of her tea.

I can't help but laugh. For one of the sweetest looking people I've ever seen, Winifred apparently takes no shit.

"And on top of that, I can't, for the life of me, find Captain," Winifred says.

"Captain?" I ask.

"My familiar, darling. Captain is my squirrel. About yea big." Winifred's hand shapes the size of an invisible football. "Fluffy red tail. Has a tendency to bite without warning. Do shout if you see him."

"S-Sure." I'm unable to form a logical sentence as a young man enters the store, takes off his cap, and nods politely in our direction. He's a few years older than me, I suspect. Weather-beaten with stubble around his chin.

"Hello," he says, taking his cap off.

Gran and Winifred stand and make their way over to him.

Gran is all business as she places her palms on the counter and smiles. "What can we do you for?"

The man fiddles with his cap. "It's the wind and the fish."

"Oh, tell me about it," Winifred chimes in. "I've had the hot breath of an angry pirate tooting out of my rectum since last night's dinner."

I nearly spit my tea across the room.

"Winifred," Gran says, her eyes unblinking, "kindly stop talking."

The fisherman stifles a laugh.

"This gentleman is talking of the harbor, I assume. Not your ghastly bowels."

Winifred seems stunned for a moment, her mouth gaping open like a fish out of water as Aggie continues.

"Correct me if I'm wrong, sailor boy, but I'm thinking you're after more than just a strong cup of tea?" Gran says with a wink. "Win, whip us up a spice bag." Gran turns to consult the array of bottled goods behind her. "We'll need two spoonfuls of Devil's Dung, a heap of sweet laurel, a sprinkle of Jamaica pepper." Gran is in her element, and I can't help but smile. "Aaand… one string of dried sea banana."

Winifred busies herself and adds the ingredients into a small muslin bag, then ties it with some twine.

Gran hands the fisherman the bag. "This will help attract the fish. Soak the spice bag in warm water overnight, then pour half of the liquid off the bow of the boat before casting off."

The fisherman nods, as if all of this is perfectly normal.

"Then dip the brush once into the ocean and once into the spice liquid," Gran says, opening a drawer beneath the counter and retrieving a paintbrush.

The fisherman takes mental notes as Winifred plonks down in her pink armchair next to me again, clearly peeved at Gran's bowel insult.

"You then must paint a circle onto the sail counterclockwise with the remaining residue, ten to fifteen minutes before you'd like to sail off. This will attract the wind." Gran nods and clasps her hands together.

"Thanks, Aggie," the fisherman says, taking out his wallet.

"Oh, no, don't be daft," Gran says. "Fishing is what keeps our little town putting along. This is on us. Just remember to drop by next time and buy some Earl Grey."

Winifred rolls her eyes, taking a sip of her tea as the fisherman leaves—he's smiling like he's just been given a bag of gold.

Gran joins us and pats my arm tenderly, glancing over at Winifred, who is avoiding eye contact. "Come on then, Win, let's have it," Gran says with half a smile.

"You'll be eating out of a dumpster if you keep on offering up goods without payment," Winifred says.

"Not a chance," Gran says with a giggle. "Besides, if we ever get too famished, we can always roast old Captain. Squirrel is a delicacy."

I snort-laugh.

Winifred opens her mouth to retaliate when a red-tailed squirrel climbs up her armchair and sits on her shoulder. "There you are!"

"On that note," I say, standing, "I'm going to go for a bit of an explore. That OK, Gran?"

Gran nods as I give her a kiss on the cheek.

"See you soon, Winifred."

I give her a kiss on the cheek too before stepping out into the crisp afternoon sun. Making my way back toward the harbor, the uneven cobblestones turn my calves to lead. I pass a few old trinket shops, Joanne's Herbal Cleaning Supplies, Codswallop Fish n' Chips, and a few dilapidated old buildings with empty interiors.

I turn a corner near the post office and spot Dorset Harbor High sitting between two giant Norway maple trees. I take a deep breath of seaside air as the seagulls fly in circles above. As good as it is to be spending time with Gran, I'm genuinely petrified about starting over and meeting new people senior year. Nobody likes being the new guy. Especially during the last year of school.

I put my hands in my pockets and dawdle farther down the street toward the water when I see him. A guy, roughly my age, staring out at the ocean. His legs dangle on either side of a limestone wall that's crumbling at the edges. He has light brown hair and a jawline for days.

For the briefest moment, he looks up at me and I notice the faintest tinge of a smile on his lips. He holds my gaze for a moment with his gorgeous eyes, one brown eye and one green, before he turns back to stare at the sea.

My heart rattles around my ribcage, and I think back to what Gran said at the pub. *I have a sense when love is on the horizon...*

Maybe moving here won't be so bad here after all.

Three

RAIN. A PERFECT MOOD FOR the impending doom I'm feeling about my first day at Dorset Harbor High. The cascading waterfall batters the window and rattles the roof as I crawl out of bed and rummage around my drawers. I want a cute outfit, something that gives me a low profile in case I bump into the tall, dark, and handsome chameleon-eyed guy I saw at the harbor yesterday. Eventually I decide on a simple white tee and jeans. How very basic, I know.

When I arrive in the kitchen, Gran is giving Newt peanut butter out of the jar and humming to herself.

"Hiya, my sweet," she says, throwing the jar into the bin with a clang. "Excited for your first day?"

I shrug, feeling an all-encompassing anxiety that burns through my veins.

"Remember darling, you're a gifted one. Tomkin's grand-daughter will keep an eye on you. Just remember to be yourself."

I chuckle. That seems to be the standard line for parents and grandparents whenever they're explaining how to get along in life. If only it were that simple.

Gran rubs her hands together and smiles. "Before you go, what do you say we give your powers a crack?"

"Uh, sure?" I say, rocking back and forth on my heels.

"Let's tidy your room."

"I've made my bed already."

"Great! Let me go and mess it up so we can redo it!"

Weird, yes. But then again, so is everything else that's happened in the last twenty-four hours, so I stand and follow her up to my room.

Gran throws her arm around me. "You're a regular Marie Kondo, aren't you? Please don't hate me for doing this." She clicks her fingers and my room shudders like it's been hit by an earthquake. The cupboard explodes open. My suitcase unzips itself and throws itself against the headboard of my bed. The bed kicks itself apart as blankets go flying. The chest of drawers that I'd carefully put my clothes away into fling open as a pair of my undies ricochet off the ceiling lamp.

"What the f—"

"Find all of your underwear in the next thirty seconds, and I'll pay your college tuition." Gran giggles like it's the funniest thing in the world that my room has just been torn apart by an invisible King Kong.

"Gran, what *was* that?" I ask. I'm trembling. "Are all your powers, um, so—"

"Fabulous? Yes." She does a spin like she's part of the New York City Ballet and curtsies. "Now, let's clean this room."

I go to pick up the mess that's strewn around as my undies fall from the ceiling lamp.

"I mean, with your gift," she says with a wink.

"OK, I need to be honest with you, Gran. I don't think I have, um, whatever it is that you have."

"Bollocks," Gran says, which makes me scoff. "You're a Silver," she adds with a nod, like it's settled. "And you'll soon learn how to use your abilities constructively. Now tell me, have you ever felt a strange sensation in the pit of your stomach?"

I can't help but laugh. "Um, I guess?"

"It's a bit like lightning in your belly. Or diarrhea. It depends on your mood."

How in the hell are we talking about diarrhea before midday?

"What I mean is, it's all-encompassing. You feel it within you. You know that you hold a certain power within that needs to be unleashed."

I nod. I know what she's talking about. Right before anything weird has happened before, I've always felt like I'm at the top of a rollercoaster, just about to drop. I used to feel like that with my ex-boyfriend too, only that rollercoaster derailed and ruined me in the process.

"Well, what I want you to do is find that power and catch it. Hold onto it, harness it, and then focus." Gran has this calm about her that makes me feel like I'm the only person on the planet. "You find it," she explains and closes her eyes. She takes her teaspoon from an inside pocket. It looks shinier than I remembered, sort of like it's glowing. "Harness it," she continues as she turns slightly toward the cupboard, "and focus."

With a pop, the cupboard rattles as the suitcase lifts into the air, zips closed, and hurls itself inside, the two doors clicking shut behind it.

Gran smiles and shrugs, as if she's just boiled the kettle. "Now you try."

I take a breath. "Do I need the... spoon?"

Gran smiles. "Not yet."

I take another breath.

"Now. Focus."

I wait for the faintest tingle to occur and try to latch onto it. It starts like the flutter of wings. A cold breath of air makes itself known in the pit of my stomach, and I attempt to focus. I breathe again and hone my attention to the bed. The corner of the ruffled blanket begins to flicker, like a small breeze has entered through the window. I concentrate harder, and the blanket ripples some more, then catapults itself at the headboard, landing in a crumpled mess.

"A perfect start."

IT'S STILL RAINING WHEN GRAN pulls up out front of Dorset Harbor High. A few people mill about, attempting to conceal the cigarettes they're smoking.

I grab my backpack from the backseat. "Thanks for the lift."

"Ooh, wait," Gran says. She hands me a paper bag. "Some lunch."

I smile. Inside is a sandwich, a bottle of home-brewed iced tea, and three custard creams.

"Thanks." I give her a peck on the cheek and step out into the drizzle.

I make my way through the throng of people in the entrance hallway as a girl roughly my age hands me a flyer.

MARCUS BRIGHT
MISSING SINCE SATURDAY, 19TH OCTOBER
ANY INFORMATION PLEASE CONTACT DORSET POLICE

A missing teenager? Seriously? Where the hell have I moved to?

I fold the flyer and put it in my back pocket and walk toward the administration desk.

A young woman with a badge that reads MISS FERRIS sits behind the glass divider. She looks bored as hell and in no mood to talk as she scrolls through her phone, occasionally blowing a giant purple bubble from the gum she is chewing, like it's the last piece of food on earth.

I feign my best "nice to meet you" smile and knock lightly on the glass window. "H-Hi, I'm... My name's Felix Silver. It's my first day and—"

"Fill these out," Miss Ferris says, throwing a manilla folder in my direction through the letterbox on the window.

I find myself a seat nearby and take a pencil from my bag.

Once I'm done, I slide the folder through the glass to an uninterested Miss Ferris.

"Silver?" she asks with a yawn.

"Yes."

"Your gran is a good egg. Helped me out a few months back with my dodgy knee."

I don't know if Miss Ferris is talking to me directly or just in general. She's not making eye contact but is instead playing what I think is Candy Crush on her phone.

"Great. That's, uh… Do you know where my first class is?"

Miss Ferris inhales slowly and looks underneath her desk, flicking through separators until she finds another, almost identical, manila folder. "Geography with Mr. Jordan. B Block."

"Thanks." I take the folder, which includes my timetable, locker number, and a guidance counselor booklet.

I head in the direction of B Block, which is thankfully signposted, and find a seat at the back of the class.

Our teacher arrives shortly after, a small and stout man with an intense mustache that belongs in vintage porn. The other students quiet down as a few last-minute stray notes are handed across aisles.

"Before we begin, I'd like to mention, once again, that the police are appealing to anyone who may have any information about the disappearance of Mr. Bright. Please make yourselves known. Marcus has been a fantastic student of mine since seventh grade, and his family are distraught."

I shuffle in my seat. A few others look around solemnly, the air colder than it was a moment before.

"Now, in lighter news, we have a new student joining us, Mr. Felix Silver."

Ugh. Why do teachers do this? Not only is it cringe to have to be the new guy starting senior year, but now I have to smile and wave like I'm five years old. Thankfully, he doesn't make me stand and give a rundown of where I've come from, but I shrink into my seat regardless and bow my head as we're instructed to turn to page forty-six in our textbooks.

After geography, I have math, which I used to struggle through back in Oakington. Somehow, I don't spontaneously combust at the sight of the Pythagorean theorem, and the class zips by quickly, followed by lunch.

I find myself a table out of the way and open up the paper bag from Gran. I tuck into a custard cream first, followed by my sandwich.

I'm two bites in when I feel a poke in my shoulder. A girl stands smiling at me, brushing her dark hair from her eyes. She's flanked by a shy-looking guy with glasses and a part in his hair.

"Fern," the girl says.

"Felix," I say, shaking her outstretched hand.

"This is Charlie," Fern says, motioning to the guy behind her, who shakes my hand and then puts both of his back in his pockets.

The two of them look like they've just stepped out of an '80s movie. Fern wears a waistcoat over a David Bowie singlet; with his glasses, parted hair, and blazer with elbow pads, Charlie looks like he belongs on the stock exchange.

They're the real deal.

"My granddad told me about you," Fern says, taking a seat opposite me. Charlie lingers for a moment before sitting down next to her, biting a nail on his pinky.

"Your granddad?"

"Tomkin? The librarian. He said he bumped into you and Aggie yesterday at the market?"

"Right, the turtle guy! I mean, um, Melon, right? His f—"

Fern nods. "Familiar, yep. Melon's a cutie." She pulls out a sandwich from her backpack and takes a bite.

"How did you know?" I ask, checking to see I didn't have a name tag on my shirt.

"She's got the gift," Charlie chimes in quietly. "Like you, right?"

I smile. "You mean I'm not the only one around here who can do weird shit without a clue how?"

"Oh, no, you are," Fern says. "I, on the other hand, have full control of my abilities. But no, I guessed because you have Aggie's eyes."

Charlie chuckles and sits a little taller.

"So, uh, how do you know how to do magic?" I ask.

"A lot of practice," Fern says.

Fern peers over my shoulder and scrunches up her forehead. I turn and look to find four girls strutting across the basketball court looking like they're on a *Vogue* runway. Each of them has peroxide-blonde hair, fluorescent green-apple nail varnish, and a silver bangle on their right wrist.

"Not a fan?" I ask.

"Dorset High's equivalent to the four horsemen of the apocalypse," Fern says. "They're just… not the greatest."

I nod. I know the type. Queens of the campus. They peak in high school, then live for the times they can return for a reunion and relive their glory days.

"Can you do magic too?" I ask Charlie. I feel so weird talking about this stuff.

Though I'm still learning to control my powers, it can feel pretty lonely not having anyone else to relate to. Mum never uses her magic around the house, and I only found out she and Dad even possessed powers when I started displaying mine. This is the first time in I don't remember how long that I feel like I belong somewhere.

Charlie shifts in his seat and scratches his dark, messy hair.

"I'm learning," he says. "Want to see?"

He's eager, and I'm in no position to judge whatsoever. "Of course," I say.

He stands up and readies himself, like he's going into battle. Fern smiles, which borders on a giggle, and cups her hand to her mouth to avoid a rogue laugh.

Charlie takes three slow, deep breaths and points at his rucksack.

I look and wait.

Nothing.

He blinks a couple of times and then readies himself again, this time with more intensity.

"I'm just…" he starts, looking between Fern and me, then focusing again.

With another jab of his finger, he points again at his rucksack, and I catch a glimpse of Fern scratching her nose twice, with intent. The rucksack shuffles twice and leaps toward Charlie's outstretched arm, knocking him back slightly before dangling on his shoulder.

He's ecstatic as he gives two fist-pump bicep curls on his lanky arm. "I did it!"

"You sure did," Fern says.

Charlie struts back to his seat as I whisper to Fern, "How long have you been helping him out?"

"Solid two years. I've never had the heart to tell him," Fern whispers back before throwing an arm around Charlie's shoulder.

We exchange numbers before the bell rings, and we head back to our classes for the afternoon. I'm not in any classes with either of them for the remainder of the day, but we agree to meet up at my locker after the final bell.

My last class is English, which is my favorite. We're asked to write a report on someone in history who rocked the boat in literature. I'm tossing up between Alan Down's *The Velvet Rage* or *The Dancer from the Dance* by Andrew Holleran, two queer books I read around the time I first realized I was into guys. Then I think otherwise. I don't really feel like revealing that part of myself just yet.

I get to my locker and throw my textbooks in. I'm taping my timetable to the inside door of my locker when I feel a tap on my shoulder.

I turn, expecting to see Fern or Charlie as planned, but instead I'm hit with those eyes.

One brown, one green.

Four

"Hey," he says, outstretching his hand. "I'm Aero."

My stomach does a backflip and I suddenly forget how to speak. The silence is deafening.

"The harbor," I say, then shake my head and stutter. "I mean, at the, uh... You were—"

Aero smiles, and I'm hit with another kick in the stomach. Only it's a gentle kick, with a feather. That is made of lightning. Help me.

"I'm Aero," he says again, his hand still outstretched.

I take it and shake way too hard. Trying to remember what my dad always said about how important a good handshake is. I think I may have broken his knuckles.

"Hello," I say. "Hello." What in the fuck is wrong with me? "Felix." There we go. "My name is Felix."

Please, make it stop.

Thankfully, Fern and Charlie arrive, and I take a breath for the first time since Aero tapped me on the shoulder.

"Hey," Fern says.

Charlie waves.

"Hi," I say, smiling, then holding the smile and wondering why my face has frozen solid. Is there some weird magic going on, or am I just losing it?

"Hey, Aero," Fern says, looking between us both and my weird, ventriloquist-like smile. "You OK, Felix?"

"Totally," I say, nodding aggressively. "I was just saying hey. Are *you* OK?" I realize how aggressive that sounded only after the words have left my lips.

Fern just giggles. "We're heading into town to get fish-and-chips. You in?"

"Sure," I say, looking to Aero. I hope the invite is for him as well.

"I wish I could, but I've got a thing," Aero says, and flashes me that ridiculous smile again.

"Felix?" says a wobbly, high-pitched Bristol accent I haven't heard before.

A young woman, a teacher, skips toward us, beaming.

"Hi, Miss Meadow," Charlie says.

"Hi," I say, taking notice of a daisy-chain necklace she's rocking.

"I'm heading to the Silver Teacup. Your grandmother has asked me bring you along with me," Miss Meadow says.

Miss Meadow is the human equivalent of a sunflower. She's all smiles. Her hair is tied up with two pigtails that sprout from either side of her head like antennas, and she's rocking on her feet like she's one of us kids.

"Oh, sure. I was just going to get fish with Fern and Charlie and—"

"Ohhhh, I love fish," Miss Meadow says. "But I'm under strict orders to bring you to the Silver Teacup."

"All good," I say.

Fern and Charlie throw me a smile before they head off through the double doors into the cool afternoon air.

"I'll see you around," Aero says. I feel both deflated and relieved at the same time. At least I won't have to hold my breath any longer.

"WOULD YOU LIKE A SLICE of bread?" Miss Meadow asks as she takes two dry pieces from her purse as we make our way up the hill.

I take an unbuttered crust from her. "Oh, um, sure."

Miss Meadow walks like the ground is covered in flowers she's afraid to crush.

"If it's good for my dear friend Robin, it's good for me." Miss Meadow tears off a piece of bread and pops it in her mouth.

Just as I'm wondering who the hell Robin is, a small bird flutters onto Miss Meadow's shoulder.

"Hello, my little gobble-guts," she says, scratching its red breast.

"Wait! Is this your familiar?" I ask. "You're magic too?"

"Just call me Merlin Meadow," Miss Meadow says, chuckling. "Not really, I'm Wendy."

I nod, concealing a laugh.

"But my grandfather was Merlin," she says, nodding as if there needn't be any more to it.

"Hang on," I say. "As in *the* Merlin? Like, sword-in-the-stone guy?"

Wendy looks confused for a moment, then nods again, tearing off another piece of bread for Robin.

When we get to the Silver Teacup, Winifred is standing outside, gazing up at the sky. Captain the squirrel dances around her feet. "Glorious day, isn't it?"

Winifred gives me a hug like I'm her own grandson and looks to Miss Meadow.

"Don't tell me," Winifred says. "Wendy has given you the old 'My grandfather was Merlin' codswallop?"

I look to Wendy, whose mouth has just dropped.

"He *was* Merlin," Wendy says, biting a nail. "You're just jealous because you don't have any famous family members."

"Darling," Winifred says. "Yes, your grandfather was *named* Merlin, however, he ran a used car garage down on the high street and could only do magic after four pints of Guinness."

I chuckle as Winifred leads us indoors, giving Wendy a peck on the cheek in goodwill. Gran is nowhere to be seen, but the sitting area has been arranged with six armchairs around a table, which is set for tea. I find a plush blue velvet chair and plonk myself down.

My phone vibrates.

Fern: You're missing out

Fern follows up her text with a selfie of her, Charlie, and a box of fish-and-chips.

Jealous, I type back.

At least I can tick off *make friends* from my list of things to do. OK, I don't actually have a list. That'd be weird. But if I did, I could tick it off.

"Oh, for *heaven's sake*," Winifred says. "Must you bring that obnoxious beast to *all* of our meetings?"

Newt bounds over to me and jumps up, paws and all, to give me a slobbery kiss that drenches my face and arms.

"Win, if I have to put up with that malodorous gerbil of yours, then you can endure Newt for an hour," Gran says. She turns the sign in the window to CLOSED and makes a beeline for me. "Spud!" Gran says, pecking me on the cheek. "Tell me all. Did you make friends? Have you fallen in love?" She gasps. "Are you pregnant?"

I scoff. "Yes, no, and absolutely not."

Newt sniffs my elbow like he's looking for truffles.

The door opens behind us, and a woman crosses the threshold and takes off her coat.

Gran turns to look. "Demelza. Fabulous to see you."

I'm introduced to her in the way most grandchildren are introduced: "I've heard so much about you" and "You're just as handsome in real life" and all that.

Demelza is tall and Black with eyes that envelop you when you look at her. A toucan with a beak that looks like it could glow in the dark sits on her shoulder.

Wendy putters nearby, looking noticeably timid, as if she's waiting for a piano to fall through the ceiling. "It's come over all cloudy out there," she says as she finds a mustard armchair to sit in.

Everyone eventually rustles themselves a seat, and Gran pours the tea. It takes me a second to realize that for each cup, a different aroma, color, and brew pours from the spout.

"I'm sure you've all met Felix by now," Gran says, beaming. "I wanted to bring him along today so he can see what we gals get up to and get a grasp on the varieties of magic and how we do things."

Wendy smiles at me, and my cheeks warm. I'm not one for being the center of attention.

"I also thought it'd be good for us to discuss the m—"

The door creaks open again, and Tomkin bustles in.

"I'm sorry I'm late, gals. It's like a Tennessee tornado out there." His accent is endearing. "Nearly blew the damn whiskers outta my chin. What'd I miss?" He takes a seat next to Wendy and neatly folds his hands in his lap.

Gran passes him his teacup, which she's just filled, and claps her hands. "So, my loves, I'm glad you're all here."

I turn and look at Demelza. She shines her piercing eyes around the room, still and unyielding.

"It's good to see you too, Aggie," Demelza says.

"So, how have we all been getting on?" Gran asks, taking a sip of her peppermint tea.

"The library was in chaos up until yesterday," Tomkin says. "Constant chatter, unreturned books, and a ceiling leak from that storm we had last week." He sits upright on his cushion, shaking his head. "I put a quiet spell in the curtains, and I patched up the leak with some beeswax and witch hazel. Just doing my bit."

Gran smiles. "Anyone else?"

"I helped the bakery," Winifred says, smiling. "They were out of flour, so I gave them a bag of mine."

"Win, as generous as that is, we're talking of ways our magic has helped Dorset Harbor."

"If you had let me finish, you would have learned that I had put an overflow spell on my bag of flour, making it never run out," Winifred says huffily.

Gran pats her hand gently and smiles.

"Sorry," I say, "But what is this?"

Demelza grins, and suddenly I'm embarrassed.

"Dorset Harbor has always been our safe space," Gran says, glancing between me and the others. "We have traveled far and wide throughout centuries to find a place where we are welcome. A place where we can be who we are without fear of upsetting non-magic folk."

The others nod in agreement.

"Here, we have found that safe harbor. Here, we are a part of a community that embraces us. We meet to discuss the ways we are helping to give back."

I look to Demelza again, unable to take my eyes off her. She's enchanting, just sitting still. She wears a flowing linen jacket embellished with small crystals, a ring on each pinky finger encrusted with what look to be onyx and obsidian, and plum lipstick that complements her olive eye shadow.

"So, OK," I say, unable to think of anything else to add.

"I have something," Demelza says, and I hold my breath.

Gran looks to her and raises an eyebrow.

"Marcus Bright went missing five days ago, and so far, the police have been useless," Demelza starts. "I did some digging and found that his last movements before he disappeared were at the Pigeon Point Lighthouse, around mid-afternoon on Saturday the nineteenth of October."

"How do you know that?" Winifred asks as Captain perches on the arm of her chair.

Demelza takes a sip of her tea. "He posted a photo on social media at 3:48 PM. No caption. Just a photo of the lighthouse."

"Is... has anyone else gone missing?" I ask.

"Not in years," Tomkin says, shaking his head.

"Was he depressed? Could he have, you know..." I start.

"It's something else," Demelza says, addressing the room. "I can feel it. I haven't felt darkness like this for some time."

"For some time?" I ask. The glances between the adults make me feel like I'm five years old and not privy to the grown-up talk.

"We had an incident. Maybe fifteen years ago?" Gran asks the room, acknowledging me simultaneously. "A few people seemed to just drop off the face of the earth."

Wendy shivers.

"And what?" I ask. "Nobody ever found out what happened to them?"

"Runaways, we were told. A change of scenery. It seemed unlikely at the time, but we didn't delve much further," Gran says, then looks at Demelza.

"It's different this time," Demelza says. "It's something wicked, I can feel it."

Winifred rolls her eyes. "Oh, don't frighten the lad, he's only just got here."

"Maybe he just fancied a bit of a stroll and got lost?" Wendy says innocently, her eyes darting between all of us. "M-Maybe he went to visit a distant relative or somethin'?"

The hope in her eyes makes me want to give her a hug. By saying it out loud, it's as if it will lessen the fear that seems to have seeped in through the walls.

"Have you consulted your oracle, Dem?" Gran asks, unblinking.

"I thought I'd wait until tonight." Demelza takes a small leather pouch from her pocket. She flips the gold clasp open and retrieves a deck of old, weathered cards from within. Each one has a simple quarter moon on the back and hand painted drawings on their fronts. The drawings are detailed, but I only glimpse a few: a candle with red wax and a white flame, an eye with feathers for eyelashes, an oak tree with gold apples lining its branches.

Wendy stands. "I think I might get some air."

"Darling, it's fine," Gran says warmly, smiling at Wendy and beckoning her to sit again.

Demelza takes a breath and shuffles the cards. Then, she slowly lays the first card in front of us on the wooden chest. A white lamb with faded pink hoofs.

"Youth," Demelza says, taking another card from the deck.

A lotus flower in an emerald-green pond.

"Purity."

Demelza takes another card but doesn't put it down.

Wendy takes Tomkin's hand in hers.

I look to Gran, who isn't blinking, as if she's encouraging Demelza to go on with her presence.

"Put the card down before Wendy breaks my damn fingers," Tomkin says, his hand turning purple.

Demelza places the card down. A simple scull with green smoke trailing through the crevices where eyes should be. She looks up, and I understand before she says the word. "Death."

Five

Newt is waiting at the top of the stairs when we get home, and I'm fairly certain he has one of my shoelaces in his mouth.

Gran kicks off her shoes and walks into the coat cupboard, only to return dressed in her pajamas. She heads toward the kitchen, humming something, and I check the cupboard in case Narnia is waiting within. No dice. Just a bunch of coats and the faintest smell of burnt cinnamon.

I meet Gran in the kitchen, and she hands me a cup of tea.

"I'm sorry if tonight was a bit—"

"No," I say, taking a breath. "I mean, a missing teenager isn't exactly what I expected in my first week here—"

"Around here—" Gran starts, then stops abruptly.

"What?" I ask.

"It's just, we've always been the ones to know when darkness is near." Gran fiddles with the edge of the tablecloth, deep in thought. "I've always prided myself on that. So knowing that something is happening, but not... knowing. It's—"

My phone vibrates in my pocket.

"I feel that I've lost my touch," Gran says, almost to herself.

I get up and go to her. Her familiar scent of vanilla mixed with her perfume hits me as I wrap my arm around her shoulder.

"You could never lose your touch, Gran," I say, giving her a kiss on the cheek. "If my name isn't Felix Silver."

WHEN I GET TO MY room, I realize I was right about Newt. One of my white Converse sneakers is covered in slobber and missing a shoelace, which I'm pretty sure has made it to Newt's intestines by now. I've yet to figure out how the hell he managed it, but instead of questioning the miracle that is Newt, I get down to my boxers and throw on an old tee. I grab my phone from the pocket of my jeans and notice a text from Fern before folding myself up in my blankets and turning my bedside lamp on.

Fern: I'm going to be counting on you and your friendship with Miss Meadow the next time I cop a detention.

I smile at the thought of Miss Meadow, and then my mind turns to the events of the evening.

I open up a message box.

Felix: Hey, what's the go with the guy who's gone missing?

I can't seem to shake the image of Demelza from earlier. Her eyes staring at the cards before her. The silence that rippled across the room as she drew the last card.

The three-dot message bubble appears as Fern writes back.

Fern: Can you meet me at the Crock Pot tomorrow before school?

I wonder if she's referring to my message, or if she just wants to hang out.

Felix: Sure. :)

I hit send and turn my lamp off, and fall asleep before the light completely leaves the room.

THE CROCK POT CAFÉ IS a small hole-in-the-wall next to the coin laundry. The walls are lined with oak paneling, and a small chandelier hangs from a cracked ceiling. I find myself a table near the window and let the smell of coffee beans and two-dollar fabric softener from next door assault my nostrils. It has a cozy yet modern vibe that I'm here for.

A young waitress with cropped purple hair and a beret wanders over. "Morning, darling," she says with a smile. "What can I get ya?"

"Oh, I'm waiting for a friend. She should be here s—"

"Fern?" the waitress asks, taking out her notepad and retrieving a pencil from behind her pierced ear. "She's a regular. I know what she'll have."

I nod.

"I'm Isla," she says.

"Felix," I say. "Nice to meet you."

"And you. Coffee? Tea? Brandy?"

I chuckle.

"I'm joking, obviously," Isla says, tapping her pencil against the palm of her hand. "Our brandy is rubbish."

I glance at the menu. Does everyone here drink before noon?

"Just a black coffee, please."

"Get the waffle tower," Isla says, pointing to an item on the menu that seems to have everything and more that could ever be included in a breakfast. "It's fab."

"Done," I say, and hand her my menu.

Isla disappears behind the counter. My phone buzzes in my pocket.

Fern: Five minutes! Sorry! Car trouble. x

I start writing back as the door swings open, and I drop my phone on the table like I've been hit in the chest.

Aero walks in without noticing me and goes to the counter.

I shrink in my seat and grab my backpack with lightning speed, desperate to search my front pocket for a mint or piece of gum.

Aero orders a black coffee, and I immediately start planning our wedding.

Seriously? The one time I don't have gum and—

Aero turns, throwing his ridiculous smile my way. "Felix!"

"Hey," I say. My eyebrows take a hike to my hairline while I try to seem nonchalant.

Aero looks at his rust-colored Chelsea boots. He's wearing a perfectly tailored shirt that shows off his chest, and an emerald green handkerchief protrudes from his skintight black jeans solely as a statement.

"How are you liking the harbor?" he asks, his perfect smile still illuminating the room.

"Good, you?" I say, then dig my fingernails into my palm. "I mean, obviously you like it. 'Cause you live here and—"

Make it stop.

Aero lifts his eyes to mine and seems to chuckle under his breath. "It's… yeah. I mean, it goes all right, I guess." He shifts his weight to his other foot.

Isla arrives with my coffee and hands Aero his takeaway version.

"Thanks, Isla," Aero says. He motions to my cup. "You've got good taste."

"Yeah, you too!" I say, more enthusiastically than I hoped.

Aero frowns questioningly. I've put my foot in it and admitted that I've been watching his every move since he entered the Crock Pot.

"I mean, coffee. I'm guessing that's coffee in there? Good old cuppa joe."

It's times like these I wish my magic came in useful and would teleport me back to twenty minutes ago so I could redo this entire humiliating spectacle.

"It is," Aero says. "Would I be right in thinking you got that from your 'gift'?" He offers me a cheeky grin.

"Uhh," I start. This makes more sense than my eye-stalking, so sure. "Correct," I say. "Sorry." I blush.

"No way! I think it's awesome. I'm still learning myself, but magical hearing has never really been my strong suit."

I nod, pretending to know what he's on about.

"Is everyone around here magic?" I ask.

He grins again. "Nah, just a few of us." He takes a sip of his coffee. "That being said, Dorset Harbor is pretty progressive. The non-magic folk don't usually give us much trouble about it."

Isla returns with my waffle tower. It's humungous. A giant tower of waffles with bacon, butter and maple syrup.

"I'll leave you to your breakfast," Aero says, rolling on his heels. "Nice chatting with you."

I am tingling from the inside out. "You too."

"Maybe we could—" Aero starts, just as the door opens and Fern wanders in, looking completely disheveled.

"My car is a piece of sh—" Fern starts. "Oh, hey, Aero."

Maybe we could *what?*

"Hey, Fern," Aero says, glancing between us with a slight blush on his cheeks. "I'll see you at school."

With that he walks out, and I nearly hurl my waffle tower at Fern.

"He's *painfully* attractive," Fern says when the door behind him has closed.

"Yep." I spear a piece of asparagus with my fork while considering chasing after him to figure out what the end of his sentence was.

"Sorry again I'm late," Fern says as Isla places a mug of coffee in front of her. "And thank you for meeting me."

"Of course."

"So. The missing guy," Fern starts, taking a sip of her coffee.

I nod, unsure what to say.

"Things have been different around here lately."

"Different how? I mean, aside from a missing person," I say.

"Well, that. But the energy? I've felt it for a while. It's like the town is hiding something."

"Hiding something?"

Fern nods. "Almost like something is going on under the surface that I can't put my finger on. People seem colder. Less, I dunno... alive?"

I don't know what she's on about, so I opt for a nod instead.

"I know that something dark is involved," Fern continues, tucking a dark stray hair behind her ear.

I'm about to mention Demelza's cards when Isla arrives again with a muesli bowl.

"Here you are, love," Isla says, placing the bowl in front of Fern, who smiles.

"How've you been, Isla?" Fern asks.

"Since yesterday when you saw me?" Isla grins. "Meh."

I check my phone for the time.

"How are we traveling?" Fern asks as Isla clears away my empty plate.

"Fifteen minutes before first bell," I say, reaching down to my bag.

"I have geography."

"I have…" I say, fumbling through the contents of my bag and trying to retrieve my timetable, which appears to have crept out of my bag when I wasn't looking. "Ugh," I groan, shining my phone light in the hopes it will miraculously appear.

I dig my hand deeper into my bag and try to remember where I could've put it. I vaguely remember seeing it on my bedside table before I left this morning, but my mind is cloudy.

"You dig any further, you'll reach China," Fern says, checking her phone.

I picture the bedside drawer in my mind's eye and imagine myself touching the timetable that I can now see clearly sitting underneath a chewed-up pencil and an empty cup. Focusing more, my hand comes into view, and I touch the smoothness of the paper. With a swift movement, I pull and feel the timetable through the bottom of my bag.

"All good," I say, waving the paper in the air like a lotto ticket.

I don't think Fern realizes what just happened. Neither do I, for that matter.

WHEN WE GET TO SCHOOL, the hall is brimming with activity. I check my timetable for the first time since pulling it out of seemingly nowhere. I have history.

"I'm in B Block," I say.

Fern glimpses my timetable. "You're with Charlie." She takes some gum from her pocket and offers me a piece, which I take and plop in my mouth.

We head in opposite directions, and I eventually find my way to the classroom.

Charlie is standing outside, watching a video of talking goats on his phone and chuckling to himself.

"Hey, Charlie," I say amidst chews from my sour grape gum.

"Oh, hey," he says. "Talking goats." He motions to his phone.

I smile. Charlie is pure innocence. He'd make the perfect monk. If monks had dark parted hair and freckles.

The bell sounds, and we shuffle in and find a seat at the back of the room. I take out my textbook and survey the class, hoping Aero will appear as Charlie locks his phone and throws it in his bag.

The four girls I noticed the other day strut into the room and sit directly in front of us, their peroxide-blonde hair almost hard to look at.

"Melody, Jane, Sarah, and Fiona," Charlie says under his breath, motioning from left to right at the four almost identical teenage equivalents of *Vogue* runway models. "Otherwise known as the four—"

Fiona spins in her chair, and I half expect to turn to stone as she glares in our direction. "Four what, Charlie?" Fiona says, unblinking.

The blood drains from Charlie's face as he stutters out an incoherent babble of words.

"H-H—" I say. "I'm Felix."

Fiona eyes me up and down, still unblinking. "Good for you," she says, and turns back to face the front.

I glance at Charlie, who looks like someone has thumped him in the stomach, and smile.

"Are they… you know?"

He looks at me quizzically.

"Magic?" I finish.

"Not a drop." He sighs, letting out a gulp of air he's been holding in since Fiona turned around. "Not everyone around here is like us."

I nod and wait until he's not looking before I let myself smile. I wonder how his practice is coming along.

The classroom door opens, and Miss Meadow enters. It's good to see a familiar face. I just hope she's not going to put me on the sp—

"Hiya, Felix!" she says, waving excitedly like I'm at the opposite end of a football field.

I wave back, trying to use some of my undiscovered magic to turn invisible or create a sinkhole under my desk.

"Felix and I are best buds, aren't we!" Miss Meadow continues, placing a stack of books and a loaf of opened bread on her desk.

Fiona nudges Sarah and the others in front, and they share a snicker in my direction.

"Now," Miss Meadow continues. "Today we're going to be learning about…"

Miss Meadow scrawls SOCIAL RELATIONSHIPS IN MEDIEVAL EUROPE across the blackboard in purple chalk.

The class murmurs.

"Who can tell me what the classes within the feudal system were?" Miss Meadow says, giggling and drawing out the word "feudal" like some off-off Broadway musical.

"There were three social classes," Charlie says. "A king, a noble class, and a peasant class."

Miss Meadow claps and squeals with joy. "Yes! Now, the king not only got to wear a fancy crown and eat lots of turkey, he also owned all the available land."

Charlie grins.

"He'd then divvy up the land for his nobles to use, and then *they* would hand out their land to the peasants," Miss Meadow continues, bouncing up and down from time to time and occasionally tearing off a piece of bread to nibble.

When the bell sounds for recess, Charlie and I make our way to the quad.

Fern arrives shortly after. She slips her phone into her pocket.

"What's that look for?" Charlie asks.

Fern crinkles her forehead.

"Mind your own, Mr. Fleming," Fern says, tapping him on the nose.

Charlie pinches the bridge of his nose. "Oh, please don't tell me you're talking to Craig again."

Fern goes a light shade of scarlet before crossing her arms. "Don't go there," she says, more direct than I expected.

"He is a garbage fire of a guy, Fern," Charlie starts, just as I spot Aero making his way toward the cafeteria.

I let Fern and Charlie continue to quibble over Fern's love life as I get a surge of adrenaline and head in Aero's direction.

"H-Hey!" I half shout.

Aero turns, cupping his hand over his face to avoid the sun. His multicolored eyes widen as he recognizes me. "Felix!" he says. He flashes his smile and nearly knocks me over with it.

"This morning—" I start, looking between him and my beat-up sneakers like my neck is made of jelly.

Aero bites his lower lip to cover what I think is a smile as an announcement comes on over the school intercom.

"*Attention Dorset Harbor High. Students are asked to please report to the gymnasium immediately.*"

Six

FERN, CHARLIE, AERO, AND I find a bleacher toward the back of the grandstands as the rest of Dorset Harbor High make their way into the gymnasium auditorium. Banners are strung up from the chipped plaster walls showing off the school's football team, THE BULLDOGS.

The teachers shuffle in after the last of the students, and Miss Meadow looks like someone has told her there's a bread shortage in town.

The principal, Miss Radcliffe, makes her way to the main podium as a hush falls over the auditorium.

"What's the bet someone's set fire to the science lab again?" Fern says with a chuckle.

Charlie snickers.

"Thank you all for your patience," Miss Radcliffe starts. She grips the podium's oak to steady herself. "This is a difficult address, but one that I must make." She looks to her faculty for support. "The DHPD notified me this morning, on behalf of Miss Ellen Holloway's family, that she hasn't returned home since she left for school yesterday morning."

A low murmur erupts throughout the room.

"As you all know, Marcus Bright went missing just over a week ago, and we have been advised that this is not an unfortunate coincidence." Miss Radcliffe takes a breath, seemingly unsure how to continue. "I want…" she starts. "I need you all to have your wits about you. It's unclear at this point what is happening; however, our town has endured many hardships over the years, and I have faith that we will continue to prove our resilience in these trying times."

I look to Miss Meadow, who is visibly trembling.

"Shit," Charlie says, shaking his head slowly.

"If *anyone* has any information that could lead to the return of Miss Holloway or Mr. Bright, I urge you to come forward and make yourself known to myself or a member of the faculty. We will ensure that your anonymity is respected within the school and the DHPD."

Fern cups her hand to her mouth. "Ellen is in my geography class," she whispers.

I glance at Aero, who has gone pale and isn't blinking.

"As of now, we are starting a check-in for all students at the end of the day. You will all receive an email link, which we require you to submit upon returning home each day." Miss Radcliffe looks out across the crowd and takes another breath. "All extracurricular activities will be put on hold for the foreseeable future. This is a trying time for us here at Dorset Harbor, and I hope I can rely on your compliance." Miss Radcliffe's features soften. "Please," she says, her tone of authority shifting slightly. She shakes her head and looks at the stale white lights that hang from the ceiling. Then she nods and looks at us again, pleading with her gaze. "Be careful."

The bell sounds, and nobody moves. An eerie silence fills the room.

Miss Meadow wipes her eyes before leaving through the double doors and out into the gray day outside.

"*What* is going on?" I say, half to myself.

Aero looks at me, and some color returns to his face. He stands up and throws his backpack over his shoulder. "I have social studies."

Fern, Charlie, and I stand and make our way out into the quad.

Aero shuffles from one foot to the other before checking his phone. "Here," he says, handing his mobile to me with a blank contact open to add my details. "Maybe we could walk home together sometime?"

Fern and Charlie exchange a glance.

"To be safe, you know?" Aero continues.

Did he catch my blush? I put my number in and go to retrieve my own phone.

"I'll text you," he says. A smile lingers at the corner of his mouth.

"Sure," I say, nodding more than necessary.

Aero wanders toward C Block.

Fern smiles, like she's just learned to levitate. She looks me up and down. "Cute."

"What?" I ask.

My cheeks burn as I head to D Block for math.

The rest of the day is uneventful, and I am genuinely happy to be greeted by Newt when I walk up to Gran's porch.

I give his giant head a scratch. "Hey, Newt."

Inside, I'm instantly hit with the smell of cinnamon and cloves, and when I get to the living room, Gran is sitting next to the fire with a giant dusty book open next to her.

"Darling," Gran says, patting the cushion next to her.

I sit and take a breath as she motions to the open door. A teacup floats gently toward me moments later. I take the cup and warm my hands, letting the spicy aromas of sage, woodsmoke, and candle wax soothe me.

"There's been another—"

"Missing teen, I heard," Gran finishes, shaking her head.

We sit silently for a moment, unsure how to go on. Newt plods over and curls into a ball next to us, his enormous tail beating the purple rug beneath him to death. We both ponder quietly, the only sounds from the crackling of the fire and the light breeze from the open bay window in the hall.

I motion to the book next to Gran. "What's that?"

"This," Gran says as she heaves the leather-bound tome onto her lap, "is the Silver Family Grimoire."

She lays her bejeweled hand across its front cover. It is a dark walnut shade of leather with a crescent moon filled with small obsidian stones. Underneath the moon is a small inscription that reads SILVER in dark purple script.

"Grimoire?" I ask.

The firelight turns the obsidian bloodred.

"Spell book," Gran says with a grin. "Since the first witches of the Silver clan back in 1692, this book has held our most powerful spells, tinctures, potions, and remedies. Everything from curing a broken heart to engine oil for a broken-down Honda Civic.

This old broad has seen it all." She wallops the book with her knuckles.

"Can we try something out?" I ask. A tingling feeling grows in the pit of my stomach.

Gran raises an eyebrow and shifts in her seat to face me. "What were you thinking?"

"Anything in there to make someone fall madly in love with me?" I say, half joking.

"A fella?" Gran asks, her eyes wide and beaming. "Tell me everything." She places a warm hand on mine and grins like she just got her broomstick license renewed.

A blush creeps across my cheeks. "Just some guy at school."

"Name. Address. Height. Demeanor. *Grades*?"

I laugh and shake my head. "Is that for a spell or for you?"

"My darling, matters of the heart are best left untouched. The magic involved in those types of spells rarely turns out the way we want. Winifred can attest to that. Back in the day, she brewed a *Lover's Lick*. A potent mixture of elderberry, rose quartz, honey, and mandrake root, in the hopes that a local sailor would take notice." Gran shakes her head.

"And?" I ask, leaning toward her.

"And he did take notice. So much so, he rarely left her sight. He followed her everywhere, throwing roses from balconies, turning up with boxes and boxes of chocolates and silk scarves. At first, Win was overjoyed." Gran giggles. "But there are only so many scarves one can wear and so many roses one can carry. It became a nightmare. He would camp outside her house, reciting Keats poems until the early hours of the morning."

I laugh, even though the thought of Aero camping outside and reciting love poems to me sounds pretty great right about now.

"Eventually, she managed to reverse the spell, but he was changed. A spark gone. It wasn't the fair thing to do..." Gran thinks for a moment. "For him *or* for her."

I nod, then motion to the Grimoire. "There's a lot to it, all this hocus-pocus stuff, huh?"

"There is, darling." Gran strokes my hand. "But if you ever call it hocus-pocus again, I'll turn you into a rocking horse." She giggles hysterically to herself, but I don't think she's joking. She composes herself and adds, "Fancy some dinner?"

I nod.

Newt follows us into the kitchen, and Gran waves her wrists, the cookware listening intently as a pot fills itself with water and floats to sit atop a flame that ignites on its own.

Gran says leans against the kitchen bench and clasps her hands together. "You try. We'll make spaghetti Bolognese."

I look to the bubbling pot and back to Gran. "OK." I lift my hand the way Gran did and motion to the pantry, which stays firmly shut.

"Breathe," Gran says with a nod.

I inhale slowly and focus again on the cream-colored pantry door. I try to remember how I felt earlier this morning, when I pulled my timetable from my bag and honed my attention to the outcome I wanted. The handle on the pantry rattles twice, then stills itself again, my hand remaining in midair. I inhale again and close my eyes as a light tingle rolls across the tips of my fingernails.

"Now," Gran says.

I let go of forcing anything and feel the atoms in pantry door shift and buckle in their place. When I open my eyes, the packet of spaghetti has melted through the closed pantry door and is flying at my head. I brace myself for impact as Gran's hand grabs it just in time.

"You, Felix Silver," Gran says, taking a breath from the sprint she just took to get to me in time, "are full of surprises."

I look at her clenched hand around the packet and gulp some much-needed air.

"I'm not sure how you managed that," Gran continues. She places the packet of spaghetti on the kitchen counter. A funny look is plastered on her face, and I can't tell if she's thrilled or wants to knock me out with a frying pan. "But I am extremely…" Gran shakes her head. "Impressed."

Seven

WHEN I GET TO MY room, Newt is at my heels. He runs ahead and lands on my bed with a crash. I kick off my shoes, open my English workbook at my desk, and begin working on an essay as Newt drifts into a sleep that shakes the walls with his snores.

It has started to rain outside, and the windows take a thrashing as the night sky slowly marks its arrival. I've got to admit, I really love cozy evenings like this. Especially here with Gran and Newt. It almost makes doing my homework somewhat enjoyable as the warmth from the fireplace downstairs finally reaches my room. A floating cup of tea with a note attached that reads *Love you, x Gran* lands on my desk, not spilling a drop.

I'm on page three of my essay when my phone beeps from across the room. Newt is oblivious, his snores making the cover on the bed flutter with every breath as I take my phone from my bag.

Aero: Just wanted to make sure you're home safe and hadn't disappeared. How's your night? :)

My heart does a weird flip before settling itself nicely in my ribcage as I sit on my bed and turn on the lamp. Newt's snoring gives the rain outside a run for its money.

Felix: I am yet to disappear. :)

I cringe hard and bury my face in my pillow. Aero is clearly being cute with me, and I come across like someone who's been stuck on a desert island his entire life without social interaction of any kind.

I start typing again, then stop when I see he's doing the same.

Aero: Well, that's good. I'd hate to miss out on hanging out sometime. ;)

OK, seriously. My mind is racing and my heart is thumping, and I don't understand how Newt is able to just sit there snoring when all of this is going on.

I stand and pace, thinking of a cute way to respond, when another message appears on my screen.

Aero: Wanna get coffee in the morning?

I smile. Newt barks softly in his sleep, and I reply.

Felix: 100%

Send.

I jump from my bed, open my closet, and search through the racks of flannelette shirts and old baseball T-shirts to try to figure out what would make me look like someone Aero would want to go on a second coffee date with.

Wait, is this even a date? Is that what he was getting at?

I unlock my phone and reread the messages a few times. I have no idea. What I do know is that I am going to turn up looking as cute as I can.

So, flannelette, baseball T-shirt, or—

"Don't wear green," Gran shouts from downstairs.

I have no idea how she knows, but it's unnerving to think she can read my thoughts.

I head downstairs to find Gran sitting by the fire, a cup of tea in her hand and a tray of cookies next to her.

"How did you—"

"Just a feeling," Gran says with a smile. "But now I've got you, fancy a cookie?" Gran hands me the plate, and I take a warm cookie that has gooey caramel chunks throughout. "Before I forget, this weekend I'm taking you to the bookshop. There's plenty to learn."

I nod. The warm fire flickering nearby makes my eyelids heavy.

"One for the road," I say, taking another cookie from the plate.

BY THE TIME I GET to the Crock Pot Café, a wind is ripping through the banner over the window. I press the door closed against the pressure of the wind and find myself a cozy seat in the corner.

Isla spots me and wanders over. She takes the pencil from behind her ear and taps it against her notepad.

"Another long black coffee?" Isla asks with a smile.

"Yes, please," I say as I look toward the door. I hope Aero hasn't been swept away with the wind.

Isla checks my glance. "Meeting Fern?"

"Aero." My cheeks burn.

Isla nods politely and suppresses a smile. "Be careful of that one. He's a heartbreaker," she says as she heads back to the counter.

I don't have time to figure out what Isla is on about—the door swings open and Aero enters, visibly ruffled from the wind yet somehow managing to still look like a Calvin Klein model.

He waves and I wave back, although a bit too aggressively. I may have dislocated my wrist.

"Hey, Felix," Aero says. He puts his backpack on the floor and sits next to me.

"Hey." I take a sip of my coffee.

"Ooft, I need one of those," Aero says, looking toward the counter at Isla, who mouths, *I'm on it.*

Aero rests his elbows on the table and looks at me intently. "How are you?"

"Good. I'm good, thanks. Yeah, it's, uh…" I don't know why I get like this around him. I've spoken to guys before. "I mean, it's weird with all the, uh, you know…"

"Missing teens?"

"Yeah, I don't really know how to wrap my head around it."

"Totally," Aero says, nodding. "I'm trying to just stay alert. I've been reading a lot, and apparently, this happened before. Three kids went missing right around the time I lost my parents. They never found out what was going on, but all of a sudden, it just stopped and—"

"I'm so sorry," I say, letting my anxiety fall away at such a heavy topic. I want to ask what happened to his parents, but don't want to pry.

"Thanks. I mean, I was, like, six, so I vaguely remember it. My nan has been looking after me since."

"I'm living with my gran right now. My parents, they're getting a divorce, so, uh… I'm sorry. I didn't mean—"

"You're cute," Aero says, and I feel my cheeks almost blister. "It's OK. Your gran is sweet. Aggie, right?"

I nod.

"I love her teas. She's always so sweet whenever I visit the shop."

I smile. Gran has that effect on people.

My phone beeps with the familiar sound of a message notification, so I check my phone. Nothing.

Aero looks at his, and I think I see an eye roll.

"All OK?" I ask.

"Yeah just… girl trouble."

I check to see if someone has entered the Crock Pot because I suddenly feel really cold, but the door is tightly shut.

"Girl trouble?" I ask.

"Ex-girlfriend. For some weird reason, she's decided to start texting me again."

"Weird."

"Totally," Aero says. His thumb hovers over his phone screen, like he may just reply.

Isla brings Aero his coffee, which he takes a sip of immediately. He then thanks her and flashes that ridiculous smile again.

"Anyway," Aero says, "not an issue. It's never going to happen… I mean, there's a reason things end. So that, uhh, new beginnings can… begin?" He smiles, a red blush creeping across his cheeks. "That's the saying, right?"

"Something like that," I say, trying to hide the disappointment in my voice. I check my phone for the time. "So, you were saying about your gran?"

"Yeah. She's been away for a while. I've been living in her place unaccompanied on and off for about two years."

"Wow."

"Yeah, I mean, she comes back often to check to make sure I haven't burnt the house down, but for the most part, I'm flying solo."

I smile, a blush creeping up my neck.

"You should come over sometime. It's pretty rad. There's a bunch of old spell books in the study and some really cool old brooms that give one hell of a ride!"

My jaw drops. "You fly?"

"Occasionally. You don't?"

I bark out a laugh. "I'm *really* new to magic. Like, kindergarten new."

"Well, I'd be happy to teach you some of the basics of flying," Aero says with a grin that makes me want to climb across the table and plant one on him.

"Sounds good." I take another sip of my coffee. "I should probably head to class. I've got geography first."

"I'm in math," Aero says with a groan. "I'll walk you to your class. For safety reasons, of course."

WHEN THE FINAL BELL OF the day goes, I head toward my locker as my phone vibrates in my pocket.

Aero: Check this out.

A video of a dog eating cereal appears on my screen. I grin, then send the heart eyes reaction as Fern and Charlie appear from behind me.

"Yo," Fern says with a nod.

"Hey," I say, opening my locker and throwing some books inside.

"What's that grin on your face about?"

"Grin?"

"You know *exactly* what I'm talking about. You've got those big, goofy eyes, and your cheeks are practically sunburnt."

I scoff.

"Fine, don't tell me," Fern says jokingly. "Charlie and I are thinking of hanging. You in?"

I nod, attempting to wipe whatever trace of a grin is left on my face. "Sounds good." I throw my backpack over a shoulder and walk with them toward the exit.

"Friday, at last," Charlie says, smiling.

We exit D Block and out into the cool afternoon air. The sky is purple and full of soft pink clouds. The first few splashes of rain hit my face as my phone buzzes in my pocket again.

Gran: Off to the shop. Back a bit later. X

"Actually, would you guys be keen on heading to the Silver Teacup?" I say, putting my phone away.

"Sure! Will your gran be there?" Fern asks.

I nod.

Charlie smiles. "Epic, Old Aggie! I mean, Aggie, she's one of the greatest. I can finally learn some tricks from a real witch."

Fern scoffs. "Easy there, fanboy. I'm sure the last thing Aggie wants is someone like you hanging off of her."

I grin. "She'll be flattered."

The trees are dancing in the afternoon breeze, and I can smell the salt from the harbor as we make our way through town. A strange feeling seeps through the cracks in the cobblestones, an uneasiness I can't shake. It's probably not helping that every second telegraph pole has a MISSING sign in bold stapled across it.

Newt is sitting on the fluffy pink armchair when we arrive at the Silver Teacup, and his dozing eyes look up at us curiously as we enter.

I walk over to give him a scratch on his enormous head. "Hey, cutie."

"Darling!" Gran calls from somewhere out back. "Be with you in just a tick. I've got my hand stuck in a jar."

I laugh as Fern and Charlie find an armchair to get comfy in.

"That poxy thing," Gran says as she enters the room. She's wearing a purple corset glittered with sapphires, and her hair is in her usual messy bun. "I curse whatever idiot decided to make jars too small for hands."

Gran still has the jar lodged tight around her wrist and a thin red line circles where it appears the circulation is struggling.

"Gran, why not just use magic to get it off?" I say with a smile.

Gran huffs. "Because, my darling, one shouldn't depend on magic for everything. One must learn to live like a regular human and deal with all of life's little... irritating... Oh, sod it."

Gran blinks three times, and the jar's rim widens and falls to the floor with a smash. With a small wiggle of her pinky finger, the pieces rearrange themselves on the floor, glue back together as if nothing happened, and float up to the table.

Charlie sits, wide-eyed, and Fern suppresses a small giggle.

"Nice," I say, giving Newt an extra scratch behind the ears for good measure. "These are my friends, Fern and Charlie."

"Fan-tabee-doza to meet you, Fern and Charlie," Gran says, pulling them both in for a hug.

Fern and Charlie are clearly in love, and Charlie hasn't blinked since we got here.

"It's so lovely to—" Charlie starts.

"SNACKS!" Gran says. She bounces on her heels and exits out the back again.

"Nothing in a jar!" I shout back.

I glance between Fern and Charlie.

"OK, she is *so* cool, Felix," Fern says, shaking her head.

"Yeah, I... She's pretty great," I say.

"Great? She's phenomenal!" Charlie says.

Gran returns and arranges an assortment of goods on the table.

"OK, we have chips, some dips from the market, some maraschino cherries, a few honeycomb chocolate chunks, and, uh..." Gran scratches her nose, and a yellow teapot with daisies on one side comes hovering from out back and lands on the table, followed by three teacups and saucers. "Tea," Gran says with a nod. "Tea is a must."

"Thanks, Gran," I say, taking a honeycomb chocolate chunk and wondering what wizardry could possibly have made something so delicious.

"Excuse me, Mrs. Silver," Charlie starts.

"Who's she?" Gran asks with a chuckle.

Charlie looks suddenly confused.

"Please, just call me Aggie."

"S-Sure... Sorry. Um, so, Mrs. Aggie—"

"Just Aggie is fine," Nan says with a smile.

Charlie is acting like he's meeting Meryl Streep, and I'm here for it.

"Aggie, of course. Well, I was wondering how you learned magic? How long did it take you to master it?"

Nan grins and bites a nail on her thumb. "My darling boy, I've been doing this for a very long time. I learned from hundreds of wacky, hokey-pokey witches over the years. Some good, some not so good. Some abysmal. The thing is, when you know you've found that spark…" Nan winks at me. "It's important never to let it go."

It's a miracle Charlie is still able to move his eyes after going so long without blinking, but he manages a nod and takes a sip of his tea.

Fern sits up tall in her chair. "I have a question."

"Shoot!" Nan says.

"What are your thoughts on the missing teens around here? What should we do?"

I look over at Nan, and she's really taking the time to think about it.

"That's a very good question. But it's one I'm not entirely sure how to answer."

Charlie looks between Fern and Gran, and scratches his nose.

"I think something dark is going on," he says.

Fern rolls her eyes. "Yes, Charlie. I think that's a given."

"No, I mean, like…" Charlie lowers his voice. "Dark magic."

Gran frowns and shifts in her seat. "That may be the case. Which is why you must all perfect your skills as best you can." Gran looks at each of us slowly. "And if dark magic is involved, it's even more important we don't go digging around for things we don't want to find."

Charlie opens his mouth to say something just as Winifred comes bustling in, carrying a large paper bag filled with something that smells of cinnamon. Captain sits on her shoulder, tucking into a nut.

"That bollocking door," Winifred says. She puts the bag on the counter and surveys the room. "Sorry, didn't realize we had company."

"Win, these are Felix's friends, Fern and Charlie," Gran says, taking a sip of tea.

"How do you do?" Winifred says as Captain climbs down from her shoulder and scurries toward the back cupboard.

Fern and Charlie exchange greetings, and Winifred plonks herself down in an armchair nearby.

"Just saw Wendy at the market. She's convinced whatever's going on has something to do with vampires now," Winifred says, rolling her eyes.

I look at Gran. "Vampires?"

"Silly, really. Wendy has been convinced there's been a vampire in Dorset Harbor for years," Gran says with a chuckle.

"Only because some old fisherman gave her a hickey when she was twenty-one," Winifred chimes in.

Charlie and Fern share a smile. Gran and Winifred are next level, and I love them for it.

"Speaking of hickeys," Fern says, looking over at me and winking.

I scoff. "What?"

"How's Aero?"

"No idea," I say as my cheeks burn. "Probably out looking for another *girlfriend*."

Charlie puts down his teacup and snaps his fingers. "Anna, that's right. I forgot about her."

"Anna?" I ask.

"His ex," Fern says.

Gran is loving every second of this as she whips her head between us like a meerkat.

"Oooooh, and is Aero your new chap?" Gran asks, rubbing her hands together.

"Nope. Absolutely not. Need I remind you he had a *girlfriend?*" I say.

Now it's Fern's turn to scoff. "Umm… are you living in 1942? Never heard of bisexuality?"

OK, fair. I shuffle in my seat, suddenly sheepish.

"Well, has he dated guys before?" I ask as I try to block out Gran's piercing gaze.

Fern shakes her head. "No. Well, I mean, I think he was seeing Steven for a little while, but nothing really ever came of that and—"

"Then how—"

"How what? How do you know if he's into you?" Fern says. She rolls her eyes again. "Apart from the fact he asked for your number instead of your socials like he's in a '90s rom-com, and he's constantly staring at you? That and the blatant flirting is enough to make me put a hex on the pair of you for being too damn cute."

I blush as Gran looks over at me. She mouths, *I like her*, and winks.

The wind outside has picked up, and the windows rattle in their old timber frames.

"Ghastly weather," Winifred says, dunking a custard cream into her tea. "I dread to think of those poor missing ones out there in this."

Fern looks at the floor. *Is she thinking what I'm thinking? That we still have no idea what's going on?*

Gran clears her throat and sits upright. "I think it's time I made tracks."

"I'll walk home with you," I say, grabbing my backpack from the floor.

We all say our farewells and go out into the darkness outside. Fern, Charlie, and Winifred head down the hill, and Gran and I make our ascent toward home.

The cobblestones clack under Gran's boots, and the trees sing as the wind brushes their leaves.

"I got you something today," Gran says. She takes out a small brown parcel from her bag and hands it to me.

I smile and slowly open the paper wrapping, then read the cover out loud. "*Incantations, Herbs & Astrology*, by Cordelia Wardwell."

"That was one of the first books I read when I was learning the craft," Gran says, giving the cover a tap. "I want you to..." Gran takes a breath. "I need you to be careful."

I nod. "Thanks, Gran."

I flick through the pages and feel bursts of electricity through my fingertips.

We round the corner and approach home, the upstairs light the only thing navigating our way.

I check my phone and see a message from Aero.

Aero: Just checking in again. Home safe?

I smile and I'm about to reply when I feel Gran's hand on my arm. She has stopped walking and is staring into the front garden.

I look up, and as my eyes adjust to the darkness, I see what she sees: At least fifty small, black rabbits covering the lawn. Their red eyes are all staring vacantly at us.

Eight

THE SKY IS SLATE-GRAY AND angry when I wake up. I pull the covers up close around my face and snuggle into the soft linen, give my toes a wiggle to wake them up, and let out a yawn Newt would be proud of.

Gran is playing old Sam Cooke records downstairs, and I throw my arm out of the comfort of the blankets to retrieve my phone and check the time.

Nine after eight.

I unlock the screen. I didn't reply to Aero last night.

When Gran and I made our way through the horde of rabbits, we both came inside and suddenly felt like we'd had four Valiums and a bottle of NyQuil, so we decided to get some sleep.

I quickly open a message.

Felix: Sorry for the late reply. Haven't disappeared. Still here. :) Hope you're good. X

I hit send, then scrunch my face up so hard I make a line across my forehead. I can't believe I added an 'x' to the end of my message.

I'm about to reply something like *Oops, meant to send an emoji, ignore said x* when the typing bubble appears.

Aero: Would you maybe like to grab some food later tonight?

My stomach does the weird backflip thing again, and I forget how to breathe for a split second. Another message pops up.

Aero: X

I roll over and push my face into my pillow to let out what I can only describe as a victory squeal before I compose myself and open the message again.

Felix: I'd love that. :)

I avoid another *X*. I don't want to come across like an absolute weirdo.

We agree to meet at the White Horse tonight at seven, and I'm unsure if this is a date or if we're just two guys grabbing some food to talk about... I dunno, what two guys even talk about. If he starts up about his ex-girlfriend again, I'll set myself on fire.

I grab *Incantations, Herbs & Astrology* and go downstairs to the kitchen.

Gran sits at the kitchen bench, feeding Newt a custard cream as Sam Cooke sings about a wonderful world.

"Morning," I say. I give Newt a scratch behind the ear before I sit on a stool and pour myself a cup of tea.

Gran gives me a peck on the cheek and nods at the book under my arm. "Studying hard?"

"That's the plan for this morning."

Newt wanders over and plonks his big head in my lap.

"Check this out," I say, motioning my hand at the cupboard, which opens slowly. Gran looks on as a box of cereal comes floating over, dipping only once before it regains balance and lands softly in front of us.

"Getting good," Gran says.

"I'm keen on the chapter about protection spells." I open the book to page fifty-six and point at the heading. "It says that if I can bewitch a pebble correctly, it'll keep me safe?"

"Oooh, I'm glad you mentioned that. It's far from foolproof, but once you've mastered it, that little pebble will help give you a sense of when something's off. Like when you're somewhere you shouldn't be or near someone a little bit on the shady side."

"Gran, did you just say shady?"

Gran twiddles her thumbs. "I did. I may look old, but I'm as hip as they come."

I laugh as Newt jumps up and licks my face.

"OK, on that note, I'm going to head into town," I say, giving Newt one last scratch behind the ear.

Gran kisses my cheek. "Be safe."

THE WEATHER SEEMS TO BE holding up when I make my way toward the harbor. The sky is still gray and menacing, but there doesn't seem to be any rain on the horizon.

I pass by the Silver Teacup and see Demelza and Winifred talking inside. Demelza is biting her nails, and Winifred is tapping her foot like she's waiting for a bus. I wave but decide not to interrupt. I really don't need any more of Demelza's premonitions, at least, not today when I have my kind-of, sort-of date with Aero.

My mind runs away as I think about him. I can't help it, I'm giddy. I've felt so shut off for such a long time, but there's something different about him. Something I'm not keen on shutting out.

When I get to the harbor, the market sellers are setting up their stalls, and the fisherman are yelling across barges at one another. I find a bench overlooking the glassy surface of the harbor and open up *Incantations, Herbs & Astrology*.

I'm three pages into learning the benefits of crab apple and mugwort when my phone vibrates.

I open the message from Fern and see a photo of me sitting on this very bench, book open and concentrating. I get a tap on my shoulder, and I turn to find Fern and Charlie standing behind me, grinning.

"OK, next-level creepy," I say.

"You're welcome," Fern says, sitting down next to me as Charlie stands, rocking on his heels. "We've just come from the library."

I put my book in my backpack. "Cool, how's Tompkin?"

"Barking mad, as usual," Fern says. "We were looking at books surrounding ancient witchcraft and dark magic. Something that could explain what's going on around here."

"And?"

"And we found this," Fern says. From within her rucksack, she retrieves a dusty old book with two letters on the cover: P.H.

"A little while back—" Charlie starts.

"Like two hundred years ago—" Fern interrupts.

"Right, like two hundred years ago, there were a bunch of kids who went missing here in Dorset Harbor…"

I sit up straighter, my fingers tingling.

"The kids were never found, but the town put a witch on trial," Charlie finishes.

"For what, though?" I ask.

"That's the thing," Charlie says, looking at Fern apprehensively.

The pair of them are acting weird, and I'm not following fast enough to figure it out.

"What?" I say, harsher than I intended.

"Well... The witch they put on trial was Mirabelle Silver."

The blood rushes out of my face.

I don't know how to process everything fast enough, and Fern looks like she could punch Charlie.

"My—Gran never—She would've, I—"

"We couldn't believe it either," Fern says, looking down at the gravel beneath our feet.

"No," I say, standing. "No, my gran would've mentioned something like this. She would've said."

I feel like the earth is moving under my feet.

I open my phone and scroll to find Gran's number. "I need to ask her."

"Felix, just... just hold off on that thought," Charlie says. "We don't know what exactly happened back then, and maybe your gran doesn't either. We should wait. We should gather some more evidence and... and—"

Fern turns to me and stares, unblinking. "We don't want you getting hurt."

"My gran would never hurt me," I say, a lump forming in my throat.

As if by magic, I spot her: Gran and Miss Meadow are walking arm in arm toward the market.

Fern and Charlie follow my gaze. The three of us start walking toward them, my heart hammering against my rib cage and my mind racing a million miles an hour.

"Gran!" I shout.

"Felix, please, just, hold off for a second—" Fern starts.

"Hold off on what?" Gran says as we reach them. Either Gran has supersonic hearing or she can listen to our conversations from pretty far away.

"I... It's..." I start, but my words aren't forming.

"Hello, sunshine," Miss Meadow says. She nibbles on a piece of Turkish bread and sways in the breeze like a daffodil.

"H-Hi, Miss Meadow, it's... The thing is—"

I'm about to get my words in order when a sound like a loud megaphone comes booming down the hill.

Gran looks up toward the main part of town. "What in Merlin's beard was that?"

"Merlin was my—" Miss Meadow starts.

"Yes, Wendy, I know, I know. But I'm talking about that commotion," Gran says, pointing to where a larger group are huddled around a shopfront.

We all make our way up the hill, Charlie at the rear practicing some incantation he's working on that is supposed to help seek out evil within a crowd, when we reach where all the racket is coming from.

It's a shop front three doors down from the Silver Teacup, and it has a large banner covering the sign with a ribbon and a tassel attached for the big reveal. It seems as though half the town is here as we find a spot next to Demelza and Winifred, who both have their hands stuffed in their pockets and are barely moving.

"Dem, Win, how are you?" Gran says, shuffling Fern, Charlie, and myself forward.

Demelza stares at the sign. "Anxious, you?"

"*Another* shop?" Winifred moans. "What's the bet they sell minimalist rubbish and expensive day planners for people without jobs or responsibilities?"

Fern grins, and Charlie is still figuring out his incantation, occasionally muttering something under his breath and staring pointedly out into the crowd. He looks silly to me, but I wouldn't tell him that.

The crowd is at full capacity when we hear the first rumble of something farther up the hill.

"What now!" Winifred shrieks.

A large black limousine makes its way down the winding, cobbled street. The only thing more out of place in Dorset Harbor than a limousine would be if Mariah Carey got out of it.

When the enormous car finally arrives next to us, a silence fills the square, as if everyone has collectively held their breath.

The driver, a tall man with a black top hat and black gloves, walks around the car to the passenger's side and opens the door.

Fern looks at me and then at Charlie, who has given up on his incantation and is staring wide eyed to find out who it could be.

From the darkness within the first flicker of movement, two black rabbits jump out from inside, sitting with their ears raised next to the door.

I turn to Gran, who is just as silent as me, as a long leg wearing an emerald-green Louboutin stiletto dips itself from out of the car and onto the pavement.

Nine

A FEW PEOPLE CLOSER TO the car step back as an arm reaches for the driver for assistance.

With an elegant maneuver worthy of a Paris runway entrance, a woman stands before us at last.

A few people in front of us gasp at the sheer height of her. She could easily be six foot three, even without the stilettos. She wears a perfectly tailored pantsuit with a long dark-purple cape that falls from her shoulders like silk. Her blonde hair is slicked back without a hair out of place, and her red velvet gloves have nails added to the fingers for effect.

"Afternoon, Dorset Harbor–ians," she says, addressing the crowd.

"Does she look familiar to you?" I catch Winifred saying to Gran under her breath.

Gran shrugs a *not really* and then focuses back on the display in front of us.

"It's been a while," the tall woman says, almost to herself. "I'm Blythe, and I'm here today to launch my new shop. I feel now, more than ever, this town needs some youth in it. Some excitement. Less *Golden Girls*, more Ariana Grande latte, or whatever."

"What the bollocks is she rambling on about?" Winifred says to Gran, louder this time.

Fern giggles under her breath but quickly masks it as a coughing fit.

"So, without further ado..." Blythe makes her way over to the tassel, and with a flick of her wrist, it catches ablaze like a sparkler and fizzes across the large placard covering the entrance sign.

Once the fizzing has died down, we are all able to make out what it says.

"The March Hare Shoe Store, at your service," Blythe says. She stands with her arms above her head, posing for a few local photographers to get their snaps. "I look forward to welcoming each and every one of you."

Blythe looks at the crowd, winks, and then goes back to her car. After a moment, she turns back. "Oops, almost forgot. My second-in-command, who will be helping me run the shop when he doesn't have school, will be my grandson." She gestures for the crowd to part slightly.

Aero stands sheepishly by the entrance, his hands in his pockets and his face flushed and awkward. My jaw drops so fast, I feel it'll detach itself from my face and hang like a swing.

"Aero will be able to help with everything you need to leave my shop feeling like the youthful, powerful women of Dorset Harbor that we all know you are," Blythe says.

With that, the crowd erupts in cheers and applause.

Gran, Winifred, Demelza, Fern, Charlie, and I tap our hands lightly, still trying to grasp what just happened. Why didn't Aero mention any of this to me? Then again, we haven't really talked, not properly. But still. This is big news for the town. I would've thought I might have gotten an update before the big day.

The crowd eventually disperses, and Aero has vanished without a trace.

I look to Fern and Charlie, who both seem just as weirded out as I do.

Gran, Winifred, and Demelza are in a quiet, deep conversation next to a huddle of townspeople. I'll bring up the new information Fern and Charlie threw at me a little later when I can figure out what to say.

My phone vibrates.

Aero: Still cool for tonight? ;)

I send back three thumbs-up emojis followed by an X. I'll bring up this spectacle later.

When I look up from my screen, Gran, Winifred, and Demelza have vanished. Why do people keep doing that?

"Where'd Gran go?" I ask Fern, who is chewing a strand of her dark hair.

"She was here a second ago," Fern says, looking to Charlie.

"You still want to talk to her about—" Charlie starts.

"Yep. There's no way she would've kept something like that from me. Not with everything going on right now."

I check my phone to see if Aero has sent anything more before stuffing my hands in my pockets.

"Listen, I think you need to just process some of this. The book didn't say anything about a fair trial, Felix," Fern says.

I nod.

"Why don't we all go get some food and just debrief? We can have another look through the book for any more clues." Charlie says.

"Sure," I say.

We make our way back to town, find a corner booth at the Parlor, and order milkshakes.

"Right," Fern says, all business. She slams the book on the table, flips through its dusty pages, and opens to the passage about Mirabelle Silver. "It says here that Mirabelle was put on trial in 1693 and found guilty of witchcraft and the disappearance of twelve children. Ms. Silver claimed she was innocent in the disappearance of the children; however, she pleaded guilty to witchcraft. Her last words at the hanging were 'It was the curling woman,' giving speculation that there was another who helped her in her endeavors."

Charlie shudders and lets out a breath he seems to have been holding since Fern started talking. "The curling woman?"

"She claimed her innocence till the very end," Fern says, shaking her head. "Maybe that's why your gran never mentioned anything?"

I tap the table with my fingers, trying to think. "Twelve kids disappeared. Do you think that means there's more to come?"

Fern shrugs. "It says that similar occurrences have happened throughout Dorset Harbor's history, even as recently as 2003. I think whatever is going on seems pretty in-line with what went on back then. But what I can't figure out is *why*. Why would a witch kidnap kids?"

Our waiter, a short guy with blond ringlet curls, arrives with our milkshakes.

"Thanks," I say, and take a sip of my Banana Blitz.

"Damn, this is good," Fern says, practically guzzling her Chocolate Supreme.

I push the book toward Fern. "I need something else to think about."

"OK… Well, uh… How's… How are you liking it here?" Charlie asks.

"Apart from the missing teenagers, weird weather, and my inability to control my magic? Great," I say with a grin.

"Hey, you said you didn't want to talk about that stuff," Fern says.

"I know, I know." I look down at my milkshake. "It's just… I dunno. I'm not really sure how to do any of this."

"Well, thankfully, that's why you met us," Fern says, nodding at Charlie. "Now, let's talk about much more important things… like your love life."

I scoff.

"What?" Fern asks, eyes bulging. "If not Aero, you must have your eyes on *someone* at school. You've been here less than a week, and if my calculations are correct, that's more than enough time to fall madly in—"

"Nope," I say, a blush forming across the bridge of my nose. "Not happening. I left that behind back in Oakington."

I'm convincing myself more than anyone else. It's the truth. I don't think I can handle another disappointment in the romance department. My last relationship pulverized my heart into a gooey, gross puddle. I'm not going there again.

"What happened in Oakington? You kiss a frog? Awake from a coma by the embrace of a prince? Climb up a long blonde pigtail to reach the lass of your dreams?" Fern asks.

I can't help but laugh. "All of the above." I shake my head. "Nah, it was just... Someone kind of showed me why I shouldn't trust people."

Charlie rests his chin on the palm of his hand and leans forward.

"I'm no Romeo, but I know what you mean. Girls are an enigma I've yet to completely understand."

I shift in my seat. "Yeah—well, he found someone else."

"What did he do?" Fern asks soothingly.

I take a moment to appreciate that I have friends in Fern and Charlie. I guess I've never really had too many good friends. Acquaintances, sure. But not this. It feels pretty good.

"He... We were together for a year and a half. I thought we were good. I felt good." I shrug and shake my head. "Then one day I noticed he was chatting to some guy online."

Charlie shakes his head.

"I questioned him about it, and he said they were just online friends. Not long afterwards, he ended it. Two months later, the mystery guy online starts appearing in all his posts."

Fern leans across the table and takes my hand.

"They've been dating for a while now and... whatever. It just kinda sucked."

Charlie nods and takes a sip of his milkshake. "What an asshole."

Fern strokes my hand. "Mega asshole. Asshole of the extreme. The king of asshole mountain."

"It's... whatever. Thing is, if he'd have just talked to me and communicated I would've been open to making it work. There's so many different kinds of love. I would've been open to the idea of opening up our relationship if that's what he was thinking. I just never got that conversation."

I take a breath. "I'm not only into the vanilla Hallmark card version. I guess... I dunno. I just don't think I'm ready for another disappointment, you know?"

Fern smiles warmly, and I suddenly realize something. I've got friends. Among all this insanity, the spells, the disappearing teens, and the weird occurrences, I have friends.

The blond waiter appears again with our plate of mozzarella sticks and sets them on the table in front of us.

"Thanks," I say, grabbing an extra cheesy stick and taking a stringy bite. "What about you two?"

"No time for dating," Fern says, almost proudly. "If I want to become a fully-fledged witch by the time I'm twenty, love is on the back burner."

Charlie looks at her, and I swear I see a glimmer of disappointment in his eyes. "Yeah. Single. Uno. Riding solo," he says, taking a bite of a mozzarella stick.

"Look at us!" Fern says, nudging into Charlie. "The three spinsters. We should start our own coven."

I chuckle.

The light fades outside as a cloud blocks what little sun was making an appearance.

Fern drums her hands on the table. "Right, I'm thinking we all take our mind off everything that's going on tonight and watch old movies at mine. We could—"

"I have a... I'm meeting up with Aero tonight, so I can't," I say, almost to my milkshake.

Fern's eyebrows shoot to her forehead. "Oh yeah?" She winks.

"What?" I ask, higher pitched than usual.

"Oh, no. No, nothing. Just... So you *are* dipping your toes back into the pond?"

I scoff. "He's a friend. We're just... We're grabbing some food, that's it."

"Uh-huh," Fern says, rolling her eyes. "Well, you don't need magic to decipher that look on your face."

"What look?"

"Starry-eyed. Dreamy. Thinking of all the ways you could plant one on him."

Charlie laughs.

"Stop," I say. "I am one hundred percent *not* thinking that."

OK, that was a lie, but unless she can read my—

"I can," Fern says innocently. "I mean, not well. But I know that you're lying through those perfect teeth of yours."

Charlie looks at me and shrugs. "Don't worry. I'm not on her level."

I shake my head and stand. "Right, on that note, I'm heading home to take a bath."

"Enjoy your date," Fern says with a grin.

"Non-date," I say.

"Whatever you say," Charlie cuts in, winking like he's got something caught in his eye.

WHEN I GET HOME, GRAN is nowhere to be seen. In my bedroom, I find Newt curled under my desk and snoring. Not even the apocalypse could wake that dog.

I throw my bag on my bed and head to the bathroom. The big copper bathtub sits atop white tiles. The window overlooking the backyard gives me a front-row view of the oak tree swaying in the afternoon breeze.

I raise my hands at the tub and focus. "OK, let's give this a go."

The faucet sits silently, looking at me like I'm an idiot who has no business doing magic.

I crack my neck and shake it out.

When I raise my hands again, I feel the tiniest prickle of electricity in the tips of my fingers.

I hold my hands steady and watch the faucet, imagining it turning, the water spilling out and filling the tub.

A drip splashes into the copper tub, followed by a creaking sound, like all the old pipes in this house are coming alive.

I focus again as the faucet unleashes a torrent of water, splashing up the sides and settling nicely in the bottom.

With my left hand, I motion to the mason jar next to the sink. The cap swirls off and ricochets off the mirror before floating over the tub and sprinkling Gran's Boisterous Bubble Mix into the water.

Within minutes, the bath is full, and my fingers feel like they've been put in a blender, but I'm stoked! Completely and totally, overwhelmingly *stoked!*

I sink into the tub and let the warm, bubbly water soak my skin.

My mind wanders to Aero, to Gran, to the bizarre world I've been dropped into, and anxiety creeps through my veins. I'm used to anxiety. I've gone through the various stages of panic since I was a kid, but this feels different. When Mum and Dad told me they were separating, I felt anxious in a way that I hadn't before, but even that didn't hold a candle to this. It's like my head is a corridor full of overflowing rooms, and no matter how many doors I close, another crashes open.

I sink lower into the soapy water and wiggle my toes, reminding myself that I'm here. I'm here, and it's OK.

The front door downstairs opens and closes as the last of the day's light fades, and the shadows from the tree outside start to disappear with the sun.

After a solid hour of soaking in the tub, I dry myself off and get dressed. I opt for a raglan tee, some ripped jean shorts, and a pair of dusty, white Converse sneakers. After a once-over in the mirror, I decide I look decent enough and head downstairs.

The front hallway is empty except for the umbrella stand and a note poking from underneath the old crystal vase atop the hall table: *Just popped home to grab the Grimoire. Meeting Demelza for tea. See you a bit later. X*

I fold the note and put it in my back pocket. As cheesy as it is, I keep everything. Every letter, ever Christmas card, every memory I have with my family. I keep it all in my journal.

I check my phone for the time: 6:39 PM. I give Newt some chicken necks for dinner and head out into the purple evening light. I close the rickety old gate and make my way toward town. The sky is an ever-changing splash of purple, pink, and orange, and there's a faint sound of an owl somewhere overhead.

After making a left on Old Creek Road, I feel the familiar cobblestones as I see the harbor come into view around the corner.

I'm paces from the White Horse when I check my phone for the time, and a message from Aero vibrates to life on my screen.

Aero: Turn around.

Ten

I TURN TO FIND AERO slowly walking toward me. He's wearing a rust-colored flannel, some skinny jeans that make his legs look amazing, and some faded sneakers.

"Hey," he says as he gets closer.

We do this awkward half-hug that resembles two drunken T-rexes, and as we break apart, I see he's blushing.

"You look great." I am a walking cliché.

"*You* do," he says back, which tells my legs to stop working momentarily. Aero claps his hands together. "Do you like fish?"

I cup my hand to my mouth as nonchalantly as I can to see if he's referring to my breath.

"I'm not great at first dates, but if you like fish, I think I have an idea."

First date?

"I love fish," I say, looking at my boots. "And… just to clarify, this is a date?"

Aero's eyes widen, and his forehead glistens with sweat like a glazed donut before he stammers, "I mean, if… you want it to be. I… just thought that—"

"I'd love that. I guess I'm not great at first dates either." I'm unable to wipe the grin off my face.

Aero taps my foot with his and nods.

"Great. We can have a completely awful first date, and neither of us will know the difference," he says with a laugh.

We wander down toward the water as the last of the evening light dips below the cliffs.

A small stone shack with a sign atop that reads CODSWALLOP FISH 'N CHIPS in bold, rustic letters sits nestled between a laundromat and a candle store.

Aero grins and orders for us, declining when I offer him some cash for mine.

"You can buy on our second date," he says.

A swarm of fireflies has found their way to my heart.

When our food is ready, Aero leads us to a small clearing near the harbor that has a perfect view of the cliffs. The houses light up as night closes in and the dark sea ripples beneath us.

I sit cross-legged on a patch of grass. "Not bad."

Aero sits next to me and hands me my fish-and-chips.

"I have to admit," I say, taking a bite of a chip, "you're a pretty mysterious guy."

Aero frowns, looking at me like I've asked him to crack the DaVinci Code.

"I mean, your grandma turning up, you running her new store," I say, trying to push him for information.

"Ha!" Aero says, giving me a nudge with his shoulder. "I didn't even know she was back until last night. Gran's like that. Bit of a free spirit. You never know when she's gonna turn up."

"Is she... Does she have powers like us?"

"She does," Aero says, looking out across the harbor. "More powerful than most, but she rarely uses it."

"How come?" My fingertips tingle at the talk of magic.

Aero looks down. "Family history. She's never really spoken much of it. But apparently, she lost control once."

"Lost control?"

"Yeah. I mean, I don't know the full story. I've tried getting it out of her, but I've never had much luck." Aero prods the fish with his fork. "Now she just focuses on the simple stuff. A potion here or there when she's not feeling well, or the occasional exploding candle trick for birthdays."

I cough out a laugh and relax a bit. "So, what else don't I know about Aero?"

"Hmmm." Aero looks out at the cliffs and smiles.

His smile is like nothing I've ever seen. It sends shockwaves all over me and I grin at the sight of it.

"Dogs or cats?" I prompt.

"Dogs."

"Sweet or savory?"

"Savory, always. Unless it's ice cream. Then always ice cream."

"Meryl Streep or Jessica Lange?"

Aero crinkles his forehead and belts out a laugh. "Meryl. Always."

"Good answer. That was the decision-maker."

"It was, huh?" Aero says, leaning into me and making me melt all over.

I nod. "Guys or girls?"

An icy wind rips across the water.

"Uh, what?" Aero asks, sitting back and looking at me silently.

I can't believe I just said that. I try to think on my feet and remember any spells to turn back time by a fraction of a second but instead just open my mouth and wait for something to come out.

"I mean, sorry. You mentioned your ex-girlfriend… and I guess I—"

"Never heard of bisexuality?" Aero says, his voice gravelly.

"N-No, I mean, of course. I was just—"

"Just thinking that bisexuality was what? A bit of a stepping-stone to Gay Town?"

I shake my head and realize how insensitive I must seem, but he's half smiling.

"Or just confused? I've gotten that one a lot. Just a confused gay guy who hasn't made the leap yet?"

I shake my head some more, making little star flecks appear in my vision.

"I'm sorry. That was shit of me," I say, pulling out a clump of grass next to me.

Aero sits quietly for a moment. He fixes his gaze on the marbled water, then on me. "It took me a long time to understand who I was, you know?"

I nod.

"And I know it's not black-and-white, but I also know that the best things in life rarely are."

I nod again, feeling like a bobblehead in a monster truck.

"I'm truly sorry," I say.

Aero shifts his body toward me and smiles. "It's fine," he says.

The tension I've been holding in my neck releases.

"Sorry if I got worked up," he adds. "I just like you, and I guess I don't want you to not get the real me. Make sense?"

I smile, nodding once more for good measure.

A light breeze dances across the water before reaching us, causing his dark hair to flicker across his forehead.

A rustling behind us announces a guy and a girl who seem to have had the same idea as us, only with a checkered blanket to sit on and a bottle of expensive champagne to have with their fish-and-chips.

Aero looks at me and winks. "What do you reckon?" he whispers, cocking his head toward the couple. "First date?"

I shift my gaze. "Nah, wedding anniversary."

"Wedding anniversary? How many years?"

"Three. Maybe four. But he's busy with work, and she has her suspicions about his PA."

Aero laughs. "Oooh, getting juicy." He sneaks another glance at them. "But it's not his PA she needs to worry about. It's his weird addiction to eating toilet paper that could send this marriage down the tube."

I scoff. "Toilet paper addiction?"

"What? You've never seen that show about all the weird things people get addicted to?" Aero says, unable to contain his laughter. "One lady was hooked on eating chalk!"

I bury my head between my legs to avoid a snorting laugh.

The couple continue enjoying their date night, and we sit quietly for a while and look out across the harbor.

I feel comfortable. Really comfortable, for the first time in a long while. Aside from my crippling insecurities around guys and relationships, whatever it is that me and Aero are doing right now, it feels good.

After the last of the sun has disappeared, we stand and dust the grass off our legs and head back toward town.

"Thanks for tonight," Aero says, biting his lip.

I smile. The light from the White Horse gives him a glow Hollywood lighting couldn't replicate.

"Thanks to you too." As we reach the fork in the cobblestones, I add, "You're pretty great."

"I'm this way," Aero says, motioning left.

I point right. "I'm that way."

Aero nods.

I look at his perfect lips and back up to his eyes. He seems nervous. Electricity runs through my fingers, but I don't think it's magic.

"I'd like to... I'd like—" I start, gathering my thoughts. "It'd be cool to do this again."

Aero smiles, his shoulders slacking somewhat. "I'd love that." Aero leans toward me. My heart rattles against my rib cage.

I close my eyes, expecting the soft touch of his lips on mine, when a message tone cracks through the moment like a sledgehammer.

Aero fumbles in his pocket and looks at his screen, rolling his eyes. "S-Sorry," he says, shoving it back into his pocket. "Just my, uh—"

"It's cool. Thanks for a good night," I say, giving him my best attempt at a smile. "See you at school."

"Yeah," Aero says, his smile bright again. "See ya."

We turn and head in separate directions, and I wait until I'm out of sight before I let my smile fall. I know it's useless to get caught up in the fact that his ex is still messaging him when I don't even know what *we* even are, but it still stings.

I turn the corner to head up our street when I see the girl from the headland up ahead. Clearly it wasn't any kind of anniversary if she's walking home alone.

I take out my phone to text Aero to tell him, then think better of it. He's probably messaging his ex and wouldn't get much out of me letting him know about the couple from our date.

I go to put my phone back in my pocket when I hear her scream.

Eleven

THE SCREAM PIERCES THROUGH THE air like a knife, nearly making me drop my phone.

When I look back up, the girl is standing still, about a hundred meters ahead of me, her arms out on either side.

"Please," she says, her left leg trembling.

I'm frozen to the spot. I try to speak, but my mouth is dry and my vocal cords are crackled shut.

The girl takes a shuddered step back, then another. She puts her hand in front of her, as if calming a feral dog. "I just want to go home."

The darkness blocks out whatever is in front of her as I try to file through my mind to figure out a spell, any spell, even just to light up the path so I can figure out what—

A large cracking sound, like a branch breaking, fills the night air, and I catch a glimpse.

There stands a thin creature, taller than the girl but wiry like a corkscrew willow. Atop its head look to be horns, straight and pointing to the stars.

My whole body aches from standing so still. My breathing turns rapid as I stare ahead, not daring to take my eyes away yet trying to figure out what to do.

I force my legs forward, one at a time, toward the girl.

"W-Wait," I say, my voice nothing but a croak.

The creature stands motionless, and the girl slowly backs away.

Silence envelops the street as a streetlamp bulb shatters, sending sparks across the street like fireworks.

Then the scream. A guttural, inhuman scream comes from the girl as the cloaked creature runs at her.

There's a thumping, like the wind being kicked out of something, as the creature and the girl collide.

I open my mouth to scream, but nothing comes out.

The girl hits the ground like a bag of cement and is swooped up by the creature and dragged into the woods.

The quiet that engulfs me is overwhelming. Not a single tree branch moves, the leaves caught in the gutters have completely frozen in time, and the grass stands to attention like an army of soldiers.

I blink a few times to remind myself where I am, that I can still move.

When I look down at my phone in my hand, I'm shaking, almost convulsing.

Attempting to unlock my screen, I fail twice, my fingers rattling like bones.

Eventually, it unlocks after forced focus, and I stare at my screen like it's a foreign object.

I think I'm in shock because nothing is making sense. The screen is too bright, the apps all lose meaning.

I open my contacts and dial Fern, my last brain cell coming to life to push me to action.

"Ooooh, calling to tell me about your hot date?" Fern's voice cuts through the silence and jolts me back to some sort of presence. "Did you kiss? Fool around? Get N-A-K-E-D?"

I open my mouth to say something, but I can't. I don't know how to form a proper sentence. I don't know where to begin.

"Felix?" Fern says, her voice lower and steadied.

"I... The..."

It's all I can manage. I feel like I've been hit by a truck.

Fern's breath is ragged and short. "Felix, you're scaring me."

I take a few steps backward, away from where the girl was, and feel relief that my legs are working.

"A girl," I say, the air in my lungs falling out with the words.

On the other end, I hear the rattle of keys being picked up. A door slams.

"A girl, what?" Fern says as a car door opens and shuts.

"I saw it happen."

"Saw *what*, Felix? Where are you?" Fern shouts.

"Southend," I say, my voice barely a whisper. "Southend Street."

"Stay there, I'm on my way."

An engine roaring to life is the last thing I hear before she hangs up.

Within ten minutes, I'm in Fern's car. The heating is blasting, and we are parked near the Parlor.

I realize neither of us have said anything since she picked me up, but it's OK. I don't know where to begin.

I take a deep breath in and out.

Fern nods toward the Parlor. "Do you want to go in and get some food? You're so pale."

I shake my head.

"Do you want—"

"I saw someone," I say, quieter than I planned. "Something."

Fern lets my words sink in, quietly waiting for me to go on, like coaxing a dog with a biscuit.

"The something took a girl." My mouth is dry, and my head feels like a minefield. "She… I just stood there. I saw it happen, and I just stood there."

Fern's eyes are unblinking as she listens.

I explain the events of the evening. My date with Aero. Seeing the girl on her date. The scream. That horrific scream that's burned into my mind.

Fern puts her hand on mine and gently rubs my knuckles. "Do you remember what it looked like?"

"Thin," I say, nodding slowly. "Horns, I think."

"Horns?"

"I… I'm not sure. It was wiry, like a tree, but it moved so fast. It moved so fast."

I choke on the last word as a tear escapes my left eye.

My mind is running on empty, but I can't get the scream out of my head. I think of all the things I could have done, should have done, and crinkle my nose into my forehead, stopping more tears.

My phone vibrates, but I let it go to voicemail. I send Gran a text to let her know I'm OK and I'll be home soon before sinking into my seat and closing my eyes.

"What's going on?" I say, half to myself, half to Fern.

Fern lets out a long breath, then sits lower in her seat and looks over at me.

"We need to speak to the police," I say, digging my phone out of my pocket.

Fern starts her car. "And say what? That some wiry, mythical creature grabbed a girl and made her vanish without a trace? They'll think you're making it up. Or worse."

"No! They know about us! About magic, I mean… They'd listen. They *have* to listen!"

"Felix, they won't get it. Trust me on this. We need to speak to your gran."

Part Two

Together

Twelve

TYPICAL. MY FIRST DATE IN however long, and I'm interrupted by Mel.

I wait until Felix has rounded the corner before I dig my phone out of my pocket and open the message.

Mel: Please, can we just talk?

I roll my eyes and stuff my phone back in my pocket, retrieving it seconds later to reply.

I have no idea where to begin.

I take a deep breath and start typing.

Aero: You don't date someone for six months and message a bunch of guys on the side. You don't date someone and bail on them at the last minute to go get drunk with a bunch of guys from the football team.

I shake my head and delete the message. It's nothing I haven't said to her already.

I opt for something simple:

Aero: I'm sorry. I've met someone else.

Send.

Strangely, I'm relieved. There's a weird giggly feeling in the pit of my stomach, and I'm pretty sure it's because of Felix.

Ooooft. Felix.

I open my phone again to send him a goodnight message—yeah, whatever, I'm cheesy like that—when I hear something.

At first I think it's a car doing donuts somewhere nearby, until I hear it again, clearer this time.

A scream.

I look to my right at the forest that splits the town. The shrubbery and vines that cover the entryway seem menacing as I take a step into the wild.

I focus forward and mutter a light incantation that glows from my palm and helps me see the way.

A branch nearby cracks under the weight of a squirrel, and I nearly roll my ankle from panicking.

OK, maybe walking into a dark wood in the middle of the night wasn't the best idea I've had in a while, but that scream was—

I hear it again. This time it's softer, more of a moan.

I slow down and tread carefully over the brambles and leaves, lifting my legs high and placing them steadily with each step.

I defuse my light incantation and move forward into the pitch darkness.

My breathing is rapid, but I somehow manage to keep a lid on it as I push through some hanging vines and see a faint silhouette in the shadows.

I cup my hand to my mouth to stop the sound of my breath and focus my eyes into the darkness.

A girl, maybe a bit older than me, lies flat next to the trunk of an old oak. She's gasping for air and her face is scrunched up and wincing, the only light illuminating her coming from the moon.

I take a step forward to say something when I hear leaves rustle; someone walks slowly toward her. They have a feminine shape, and in their clutched, outstretched hand, something glimmers.

I turn and run. My legs burn, my chest heaves, and my forehead is doused in sweat.

When I finally make it to the main road, I collapse against a brick wall in front of an old, dilapidated shack, put my head between my knees, and focus on my breathing.

I can't think fast enough.

I let my mind settle as everything comes into focus.

The girl, her limp body against the oak, the rustle of the bushes. The woman. Is she holding something?

At first I thought it was a knife, but as my thoughts settle, the image becomes as clear as the moon above me.

Aggie, moving slowly with her arm raised, clutching her teaspoon.

Thirteen

WHEN WE ARRIVE AT HOME, the house is dark, except for the living room light. The ivy around the porch looks blue in the moonlight, and the smell of woodsmoke fills my lungs as we get out of the car and head to the house.

"Gran?" I call, my voice slightly above a whisper as Fern and I close the front door behind us.

I find her sitting by the fire, curled up and asleep in her armchair with Newt by her legs.

"Don't wake her," Fern whispers as Newt lifts his enormous head to greet us.

"I'm awake," Gran says, her eyes still shut.

Fern sits on the sofa. "Hi, Aggie."

I stand in the doorway. My nerves are shot, and I don't feel like sitting.

"Something happened," Fern continues.

Gran's eyes flick open, and she bolts upright, like she's waiting for an earthquake.

"It's fine," I say, then shake my head. "I mean, *I'm* OK."

Fern pulls a blanket from the corner of the sofa and drapes it over her legs.

"Spud, you're whiter than a right-wing Fox News host, what happened?" Gran stands up and wraps me in a hug.

I slowly tell her of the night's events before sitting on the carpet with Newt, and Gran takes her seat again by the fire. The room is quiet for a long time, the only sounds coming from the crackling fireplace and Newt's heavy breathing.

"I need to ask you something," I say, looking up at Gran, then back at Newt. His big doe eyes keep my heart rate steady. "Why have you never told me about Mirabelle Silver?"

Fern looks at me and then at Gran, and I can't decipher whether she's annoyed I mentioned anything or interested in hearing Gran's answer.

Gran nods and takes a deep breath before looking at me. "For the same reason I do most things." In the corner of her mouth, a faint smile appears. "I didn't want to worry you."

"How do you mean?" I ask.

"Witches, both good and bad, have been persecuted for centuries, in one way or another. I didn't want your first experience with magic to be filled with fear."

Newt wanders over to me and puts his enormous head in my lap.

"It's a bit late for that, Gran," I say, giving Newt a pat.

"Mirabelle was innocent. Don't ask me how I know. I just do. I know it like I know the freckles on my arm. I know it in my bones."

"So, she was set up?" Fern asks.

"Without a doubt," Gran says.

"Who?"

"Anyone's guess," Gran says, shrugging. "A witch's intention is a powerful thing. *Magic* is a powerful thing. And not to sound too nerdy, but as Spider-Man's uncle said: 'With great power comes great responsibility.'"

I smile.

"The main thing is we keep our wits about ourselves. That's all we can do." Gran stands and dusts some crumbs off her dress. "Now, you look like you could use a cuppa."

AFTER OUR TEA, COLOR FLOWS back to my cheeks and my heart settles into its regular rhythm.

I give Fern a hug goodbye, give Gran a kiss, and head up to my room. Newt bounds up the stairs in front of me and curls himself into a ball at the end of my bed.

I kick off my sneakers and crawl under the covers, the sheets warm and fresh and smelling of lavender.

I flick on my bedside lamp and unlock my phone, starting a new message to Aero, when my screen lights up with an incoming call from him.

"Hey," I say, kicking a leg out of the blanket.

"Fern just told me what happened," Aero says, his voice slightly raised.

"She was fast." I roll onto one side. "I'm fine. Just a bit shaken up."

Aero breathes slowly on the other end of the phone. "This is not OK. I just saw a post on the Dorset Harbor community Facebook group. Tabatha Smith has been reported missing by her family. Apparently the police can't do anything until it's been twenty-four hours, but it's definitely our girl. I recognized her immediately from earlier…"

I shake my head. This is too much.

"The thought of anything happening to you… It just," Aero's voice is quiet, like he's keeping something to himself. "I really like you, Felix."

My body hums, like I've just drunk a gallon of sweet tea. My toes feel like they could dance on clouds, and my smile makes my cheeks hurt.

"I really like you too."

The insecurities that are always in my peripherals slowly come into focus. My shoulders tense up. I can't get hurt again. Especially now, especially while all this is going on. So I shift to more important matters. "Whatever is going on, it's going to keep happening. Unless we stop it."

I don't know what that's going to take, but I'm hell-bent on figuring it out.

"There's something I need to—" Aero starts and stops, like the line is breaking up.

"What?" I say, and I roll onto my other side.

He takes a deep, audible breath. "Tomorrow. We'll make a plan," Aero says, his voice resolute and ready.

We hang up, and I curl myself into a ball, Newt wriggling under the blankets next to me and putting his huge head in the crook of my arm.

I close my eyes and try to drift off.

The last thing I hear is the piercing scream that won't leave my mind.

Fourteen

IT'S RAINING WHEN I FINALLY wake up. I slept about two and a half hours all night, and my eyes are puffy, like I've been attacked by two giant bees.

Newt is nowhere to be seen.

I throw my phone across my bed and pinch my eyes shut. My head throbs, and a million thoughts race through my mind.

I need to focus. I need clarity. I need...

I open my copy of *Incantations, Herbs & Astrology* and flip to the manifesting chapter on page forty-nine. I was able to pull my timetable out of my backpack at the Crock Pot without much effort, so now is a good a time as any to give it another go. The pages are worn and yellowed, smelling of dampness and sawdust, but I'm weirdly soothed by it.

After reviewing the instructions a few times, I open my bedside table drawer and put my hand inside, close my eyes, and focus. My fingers tingle a little at first, like I've put them near an open flame.

I take a deep breath in and visualize what I really need.

The bottom of the drawer slips away into nothingness, an invitation to dig deeper.

My hand reaches farther into the abyss, searching in my mind for what I'm after, as I grip my palm around the cool handle of a coffee mug.

I lift the coffee from the bedside drawer and grin like I've just... well, no metaphor needed really. I just lifted a freakin' coffee out of my bedside table!

I take a sip of the black coffee and let it enter my bloodstream. The rain batters the windows outside, and the oak tree in the back garden sways like it's in a New Orleans street parade.

I jump in the shower, throw some product in my hair, dry myself off, and open my closet.

I opt for my skinny jeans, a flannel shirt, and a warm overcoat with a hood.

Gran isn't home when I get downstairs, but the Silver Grimoire is on the kitchen bench, a cup of tea next to it.

I can't think fast enough, and my mouth is dry, so I grab myself a glass of water and an umbrella from the rack in the hall before stepping out into the miserable, rainy day outside.

I'm drenched by the time I get to the Crock Pot, even with the help of my umbrella.

Isla brings me a warm mug of coffee and a plate of dry toast quicker than humanly possible. "You OK, hun?" She shakes a purple lock of hair from her face.

I nod.

"I'll leave you to it. Holler if you need anything."

I give my hair a ruffle and put my coat on the back of my chair.

I start a new group chat with Aero, Fern, and Charlie and tell them where I am.

Within fifteen minutes, the four of us have commandeered a booth, and Isla has brought us a pot of coffee and a stack of waffles to pick at.

I don't even know how to describe how I'm feeling, so instead, I jab my fork into the waffle stack and take a bite.

Charlie is the first to fidget, his face ashen and his eyes wider than dinner plates.

"OK," Charlie says, his voice bouncy and feigning calm. "There are three missing teens, and we have no suspect."

Fern nods. Aero stares at the stack of waffles, which I push toward him.

"Listen." Fern reaches into her bag and retrieves the dusty, old book again, which I want to hurl outside into the storm.

"Not that again," I say.

"What again?" Aero asks, looking to Fern.

Fern passes the book across to him and points to the paragraph about Mirabelle.

I roll my eyes as Aero's face drops and the color leaves his cheeks.

"Felix, this is—" Aero starts.

"Ancient. It's ancient. I spoke to Gran about it last night. You were there, Fern. Why does this have anything to do with—"

"I'm saying I think we should do some more research, Felix," Fern says sternly but with a warmth that prevents me from getting pissed at her.

"When I went home last night, I did some more digging, and apparently, Mirabelle was accused of stealing the youth from children."

Charlie hasn't blinked once, and I clamp my mouth shut to let her continue.

"Local sources at the time claimed Mirabelle was planning a final incantation that would keep her young forever, but the element that was missing was the youth of a blood relative in love."

"A blood relative? You mean a child from her own family?" Aero asks, taking a sip of his coffee.

"Yeah," Fern says, looking between us.

"So, what happened?" I ask, trying not to sound interested.

Fern lowers her voice and leans in. "It didn't work. Mirabelle never had any blood relatives young enough to complete the spell."

I glance between the three of them.

"Why are we acting like Mirabelle was guilty after what my gran said last n—"

"We're not," Charlie says, blinking for the first time. "But you've got to admit, this ticks a lot of the boxes."

"What exactly are you suggesting, Charlie?" I say, my voice a hot whisper. "Are you saying my gran has something to do with this?"

Charlie shakes his head so hard, I'm worried he's going to pinch a nerve.

"No! Oh my god, no. I'm saying whatever is happening sounds similar. Whoever is doing this *could* perhaps be doing what Mirabelle was accused of." Charlie takes a deep breath and shrugs, looking to Aero and Fern for support. "I mean, it's not like we've seen Aggie doing anything weird."

Aero opens his mouth to say something, then shuts it, looking at me and then at the table, like he's trying to do a thousand-piece puzzle.

"What?" I say, more aggressively than I intended.

Aero shakes his head and opens his mouth again when our phones vibrate at the same time.

Dorset Harbor High:

Attention students. Due to the events of the last twenty-four hours, we have made the executive decision to bring forward our end of term break commencing immediately. All necessary reading materials and study guides will be emailed. Class will commence in the new year after a review of the current situation. We ask that you stay safe and vigilant during this time.

Regards, Miss M. Radcliffe
Principal

Fern looks up at the ceiling before putting her head in her hands.

"Perfect," Charlie says, rolling his eyes. "More time at home."

"On that note, I'm heading off," I say, pushing my empty glass in front of me and standing.

Aero looks up and gives me a weak smile, but I just want to leave. I don't know how to process everything that's been said, and the thought of Gran having anything to do with this makes me want to vomit.

"Are you… Are you mad at us?" Charlie says as I turn.

"No," I say, giving my best attempt at a smile. "I just need to think."

Fifteen

OK, SO THIS IS FAR from how I wanted things to go.

As Felix closes the door and heads out into the wild storm outside, Fern leans over and nudges me. I guess she's just being sweet and trying to make me feel better, but the image of Aggie and the girl is the only thing circling my mind.

"You look like you're coming down with something," Charlie says, taking a swig of his coffee. "You feeling OK?"

I shift in my seat. I've never been any good at lying, and this secret is burning a hole in my chest.

"Not really," I say, looking at anything but Fern and Charlie.

"Listen," Fern says. She's using her business-as-usual tone, and she sits up straighter. "The fact is, all the evidence is pointing to something that has happened before. That's a *good* thing. It means we're one step ahead."

Charlie sits up straighter too. It looks like he's trying to impress her, but he comes across like he's sitting on a thumbtack.

Isla arrives out of nowhere and plonks a fresh pot of coffee in front of us.

"You lot look like you're planning a murder," Isla says, picking at a chipped bit of lime-green nail polish on her thumb.

"A murder would be easier," Charlie says into his freshly poured coffee.

Isla looks between the three of us and frowns. She tucks her notepad and pen into her apron. "I know it's not really my place, but you're not meddling around with anything to do with those missing teens, are you?"

Fern scoffs, outperforming all of us. "Not a chance."

Isla bites the inside of her cheek. "I just would hate to see you lot get into any trouble. The harbor ain't as safe as it once was."

I give my best feigned smile as Isla turns and heads back behind the counter to serve a burly fisherman with a scar across his eyebrow.

I look at Fern's big, thoughtful eyes and Charlie's innocent face and floppy hair and decide I'm in good hands.

"I saw something last night," I say, pushing the last few words out like I'm giving birth.

Fern snaps her head up and stares at me so fast, I think I hear her back crack.

I lean toward them so nobody but the three of us can be heard. "I mean, I heard a scream... And then... Well, I guess it wasn't the best idea, but I... went looking and—"

The door of the Crock Pot swings open and catches me mid-sentence.

"Well, looky-here," Miss Meadow sings, bouncing over to our table and grinning. "Bloody nightmare out there. I nearly got swept into the harbor when I left me house."

Fern digs her fingernails into the cracked table.

Charlie beams and nudges Fern with his shoulder. "Hi, Miss Meadow."

"I was on my way to see Aggie and Demelza," Miss Meadow says, leaning in and tapping her nose. "Secret business."

"Oh yeah?" I ask, trying to keep my voice steady.

"Oooh yes. But I can't say any more. My big gob gets me in enough trouble as it is without me going and blabbing about secret teashop business."

I can't help but laugh. Miss Meadow is freakin' hilarious without even trying.

"I 'spect you've heard the news about school too?" Miss Meadow continues, bouncing on her heels.

We nod. Fern is looking at me like she's trying to read my thoughts.

"It'll give me time to brush up on old Merlin's sorcery, won't it?" Miss Meadow opens her handbag, tears a piece of Turkish bread, and nibbles it.

"Excuse me, but this isn't BYO," Isla says from behind the counter, glaring at Miss Meadow. "You have to order food if you plan on staying."

Miss Meadow raises her eyebrows and grimaces a grin before turning back to us. "Oopsie daisy," she says. She shuts her handbag and shrugs. "Oooh, actually, Aero, do you fancy walking with me? I've got summat I'd love to talk to you about."

Fern's eyes almost pop out of her head, and Charlie can't help but chuckle.

"Well, I was actually—"

"We were sort of in the middle of... of, um, studying!" Fern says, looking to Charlie for backup.

"Y-Yeah... We were just about to practice, um..." Charlie says hopelessly.

"It's cool, Miss Meadow. Lead the way," I say, looking back at Fern and Charlie and mouthing *I'll text you* as we head toward the front door.

Miss Meadow leans into the umbrella stand as we leave and retrieves a wonky old stick amidst the fancy steel and oak handles, and grins at me as we head out into the storm.

"M-Miss? Not to be rude, but your umbrella is missing its head," I say, trying to get my voice above the crashing thunder.

"Aero, they don't call me Merlin's granddaughter for nothin'!" Miss Meadow says, poking her wonky stick at the sky and blinking.

Just then, the tip of her stick fizzes, and a domed cloud of air froths from the end, completely covering us from the torrential rain.

Miss Meadow opens her handbag and lets Robin flutter out. He lands on her shoulder, where she feeds him a crust of bread as we make our way away from the harbor.

"OK, that's pretty awesome," I say, motioning to her stick.

We turn a corner and head past the library toward Gran's store.

I put my hands in my pockets to stop the chill. "So, what was it you wanted to talk to me about?"

"Well," Miss Meadow says in her singsong voice. "I was wonderin' if you've spent much time with Felix?"

She's a literal ray of sunshine piercing through the storm we're walking in. It's kind of infectious.

"I mean… a bit?" I try to contain the smile that creeps onto my face at the thought of him.

"'Cause, well, I been speaking with Aggie, and she wanted me to keep an eye on him," Miss Meadow says, the mention of Aggie putting an immediate cloud over the gooey feeling I had a second before.

"An eye on him?"

"Yeah. I 'spect it's just her being careful, what with all that's been going on lately. But I wanted to see if you could, I don't know… Just keep him on your radar, if you catch my drift?"

If this conversation had happened a day ago, I'd have felt really flattered and even more gooey than I already do about Felix. But that image of Aggie standing near the girl is the only thing I can think of, and it makes my hands clammy and my back itch.

"Sure," I say, looking at Miss Meadow and giving her a nod.

"Great." She claps me on the back and grins, like I've just given her the keys to a bread shop.

As we near the row of shops on the high street, Miss Meadow takes Robin and puts him back in her handbag, then turns to me and shrugs with a smile.

"Well, I best be off," she says, looking up at the gray sky and sighing.

We say goodbye, and I cross the road.

The storm is so fierce, I'm already dripping wet by the time I get underneath the awning on the other side of the road.

I give my hair a shake and whack my clothes before heading into Gran's new store.

Sixteen

WHEN I GET TO THE Silver Teacup, Winifred is bent over and peering behind the pink armchair.

I put my bag next to the counter and approach her like I would a stray cat.

"W-Winifred?" I say, quieter than normal.

"Oooft, bollocks," Winifred says, nearly taking out the small table next to it as she backs out like a lorry. "Captain is under there, and he's being an obnoxious little sh—"

"I can help." I get on all fours and put my head against the squeaky wooden floor.

Captain is huddled just out of reach, and from this angle, I'm able to get a pretty good look at him. His bushy tail is squashed under the roof of the chair, and his potbelly hangs over his little legs like a drunken sailor's.

"Here, Captain," I say, putting my hand out and clicking my tongue to get his attention.

His beady eyes stare at me as if to say, *Unless you have food, you can sod off.*

I pretend to nibble on something before showing him my hand again. "C'mon buddy."

"It's no use, Felix," Winifred says, walking behind the counter and retrieving an old broom. "He's as stubborn as his mother."

"Who's his mother?"

"Me," Winifred says. She gives the armchair a wallop with the broom, sending Captain running for his life and into her waiting hands. "Anyhoo, enough about this little blighter. How are you?" Winifred motions to a faded green armchair for me as she plonks herself down in the pink one.

I shrug. I really can't be bothered going over everything again. I need something to take my mind off it all, and Winifred and Captain are a great distraction.

"Learned any new spells?" Winifred says, pouring us a cup each from what I thought was an empty teapot.

"A few… I've been brushing up on my manifesting." I lean back into feathered pillows of the armchair.

"Given any defense tricks a crack?" Winifred says, grabbing Captain's tail as he attempts to dash off her shoulder.

"Defense tricks?"

"Nothing too involved, of course. Maybe just a temporary blindness incantation? Or a winding?"

"A winding? Winifred, I'm real amateur, remember? You're gonna have to spell it out for me."

"Winding is what it sounds like," Winifred says, taking a sip of her tea. "It knocks the wind out of your adversary. You repeat *Lotuh, Mudhar, Sereni* in your mind's eye as you focus on their stomach, then pop! They're bent over and clutching themselves like they've just had four vindaloo curries!"

I laugh, imagining the poor guy who Winifred used that spell on.

"I'll keep it in mind," I say.

"You do that." Winifred gives Captain a scratch before giving me a long, hard look. "You don't seem yourself."

I shrug.

"Boy trouble?"

"Definitely not," I say, shaking my head. After this morning, the last thing I feel like doing is planning a second date. I can't even begin to figure out what was up with Aero this morning. He barely said two words at the Crock Pot.

Winifred narrows her eyes, and the shadow of a grin comes over her face. "If it *were* boy trouble, would the boy in question be someone with a name that sounds like pharaoh?"

I really don't feel like having a conversation about my love life with Winifred and her squirrel, but I can't help but laugh.

"Potentially," I say, looking anywhere but at her. "It's… I dunno. You ever feel like you really click with someone, and then they do something that just… That makes you feel…"

"Like shit?" Winifred says bluntly. "Yep. That's part of being human. Nobody is ever going to make you happy one hundred percent of the time. But that's the fun part about getting to know someone. Figuring out what parts about them you like as well as those parts that make you want to put your head in the oven."

Winifred smiles as I take a sip of tea.

"I guess." I glance outside at the still-raging storm.

I don't know why I'm contemplating the idea of getting involved with someone now. I swore to myself I'd avoid guys like the plague after the last debacle.

"Gran coming in today?"

"I think so. She's been over at Demelza's working on…
catching up."

"Hold up, working on what? What is Gran working on with
Demelza?"

"Oh, shush. Never you mind. Fact is, she's out and about till
this afternoon, but I'll let her know you popped by," Winifred
says, clearly putting the matter to bed and, I think, telling me
it's time to leave.

I give Winifred a hug and scratch Captain behind the ears
before venturing out into the miserable weather.

When I get home, Newt is sitting on the top step, chewing
his paw.

I head to my room and flop down on my bed as Newt crawls
in beside me, and my phone vibrates.

I don't even bother looking. I throw my phone to the foot of
the bed and close my eyes.

Seventeen

I CLOSE THE DOOR BEHIND me and survey the new store, drying my feet on the doormat—matte black, with a rabbit embellished in the corner. The white walls and crystal chandelier hanging in the center of the room give it a chic vibe and make my eyes hurt.

"Hi, handsome," Gran says, standing at the counter like Cleopatra on her throne.

She's wearing a black dress with a purple velvet shawl, her nails painted lime green to match the base of her ridiculously high stilettos.

"Hi, Gran," I say, making sure not to tread mud through the porcelain-white carpet.

Gran gives me a peck on the cheek before sitting on a plush sofa and adjusting a pillow behind her back.

I have to hand it to her, the store looks pretty awesome. Most shoe stores don't have sprawling sofas to sit on to try things on, but then again, Gran never does do anything lightly.

"You look tired, Aero," Gran says, tapping the sofa for me to sit. "Here." With a click of her fingers, a small glass cup appears in her hand, filled with something light pink and sparkling. "Cream soda."

I take a sip and enjoy the frothy goodness.

"Sorry I wasn't here earlier," I say, placing the glass on a silver side table next to the sofa. "I had…"

"Don't be daft, my darling." Gran dabs the corner of her mouth with a ringed finger. "I expect all this yucky stuff with teenagers at your school is putting you a little on edge?"

I nod, taking my glass and downing the remaining cream soda.

"Well, mark my words. You are safe. I won't ever let anything happen to you," Gran says.

"Thanks," I say, looking up at the giant chandelier and wondering how many crystals are in it. "I just… Last night, I—"

The door swings open, and a drenched Fern and Charlie barge in, not wiping their feet and instead trailing a river of mud across the floor.

"There you are," Fern says, taking her coat off and giving it a shake, sending water in every direction.

Gran looks to me and smiles, giving her nose a rub as the water evaporates and the floor becomes sparkling white again.

"You never finished telling us about—" Charlie starts, but Fern lifts her hand to his arm to shush him.

"Sorry, Miss…" Fern asks, looking at Gran.

"Blythe. Just Blythe," Gran says, looking between Fern and Charlie before grinning back at me. "Friends from school?"

"Yeah," I say, looking back at the pair of them.

"Join us," Gran says, beckoning them both over. "I think he was about to tell me whatever it was he failed to tell you."

Fern and Charlie wander over, taking in the hundreds of stilettos on the shelves and the giant light fixtures.

I take a breath. "I saw something."

Gran looks at me as if for the first time. "My darling, what did you see?"

Her voice is higher than usual, more strained, like the thought of anything happening to me made her vocal cords tighten.

"A girl. I saw a girl. Screaming… And…"

Gran's eyes widen as she lifts a hand to her mouth.

"Aggie… I saw Aggie Silver near her," I say, releasing the words like a canon of hot air.

Gran sits up straighter, but her shoulders drop, like she's been holding her breath too.

Fern and Charlie don't move, their eyes bulging.

"Are you sure?" Gran says, leaning in and taking my hand. "You're certain?"

My throat goes dry. I try to bring the image back into my mind. "I mean, I think so?"

Charlie looks at Fern, who has lost all color in her cheeks.

Gran nods, tapping her cheek with her finger, a large emerald ring glimmering in the white light. "Right." Gran brushes her hair behind her ears and looks at me, not breaking eye contact. "If this is truly dark magic at play, then only us magic-folk are going to be able to stop it."

I ball my hands into fists. My stomach tightens, like I've just swallowed a gobstopper.

"You understand?" Gran says, rubbing my hand and smiling. "It's up to us."

Eighteen

I WAKE FROM MY MUCH-NEEDED nap to find that the storm outside has died down to a drizzle. Newt is fast asleep and curled into a position I can't begin to describe. He occasionally runs on the spot, dreaming.

I turn onto my side and scratch the sleep from my eyes, the afternoon light fading to dark.

My phone vibrates again from where I threw it earlier, and I crawl across the rumpled sheets to have a look.

Aero: Can I take you out for date number two? No talk of anything other than how I like your smile and your ability to pull off flannel shirts.

I grin.

As cheesy as it is, I really want to see him. Which is weird, because a second date was the last thing on my mind when I was talking to Winifred. Plus, he's not wrong about my flannel abilities.

We agree to meet at the harbor.

I get out of bed and rub Newt behind the ears; his snores are back with full force.

When I get downstairs, Gran is sitting in the living room, the Silver Grimoire open on her lap and a faux-fur blanket wrapped around her.

I wander over and sit next to her as she drapes her blanket around me and pulls me in for a hug.

"I needed that," I say, breathing in her perfume as she pecks me on the head.

Gran brushes my hair back from my eyes. "How are you feeling, Spud?"

I shrug. I need some time not talking about everything that's going on. "I'm meeting Aero tonight."

"Lovely," Gran says, sitting back and giving me a once-over. "You just be careful out there."

I nod. "Of course."

"I hear Winifred gave you some tips for defense incantations."

"Yeah, she's got the goods. I'll be fine."

"I know you will," Gran says, wrapping herself tighter with the blanket. "Now go have fun. Dance under the stars, kiss for hours, fall in love."

I laugh.

"I'll do my best."

WHEN I GET TO THE harbor, the rain has gone entirely, and the purple night sky blankets the horizon.

I get to the pebbled shore and roll my skinny jeans up to my ankles, then sit on the stone wall that gives me a first-class look out at the cerulean sea.

The fishermen nearby haul their fish and crabs into crates and buckets before getting in their rusty old vans and heading home for the night.

I focus my mind on the still water of the harbor and send a fountain of water into the sky, just to see if I can.

A few passersby look on happily as I send jets of water into the atmosphere, choreographing a show worthy of the Bellagio in Las Vegas.

"Nicely done," Aero says behind me.

I turn as he sits himself next to me.

"Hi," I say, not wanting to come across too friendly.

"Hey." He looks out as the water settles back to calm, then gives me a little nudge with his shoulder. "Very impressive."

I nod.

"I'm sorry about today."

I shrug.

"Are you mad? What am I talking about—*I'd* be mad if it was *my* great-great-grandparent accused of… well, you know." Aero is fidgety, like he's sitting on an ant nest.

"I *know* my gran doesn't have anything to do with this," I say, my voice low and steady. "I know it."

Aero turns and looks at me, opening his mouth briefly before closing it, like his words got carried away in the wind. "Fern and Charlie are worried you're mad at them," he says, finally.

"I'm not. I just don't like the direction they're going in."

"Fair, but they only want to help. They really care, you know?"

Aero's eyes are almost translucent in this light. His green one is even more striking than the brown.

"I thought the deal was no talk about this stuff?" I say, melting into the relaxing rhythm of being with him.

Aero's face lights up, a grin spreading across his perfect face. "True. Very true." He puts his hands up in surrender. "Now, to the more important stuff. Your flannel is *perfection.*"

I burst out laughing. It's really not.

"Thanks."

"No, thank *you* for dazzling me with this level of sheer fashion," he says, smiling like he's in a toothpaste commercial.

"You're welcome. You also look great," I say. There's simply no other word for it. He's wearing skinny black jeans with small rips around the knees, a simple red tee, and a peacoat.

"Ready for our date?" he says, bouncing his eyebrows up and down.

I look out at the view again. "This isn't it?"

"Nope. Although I did enjoy your *Fantasia* performance with the water just now. You're getting good." He points at the vast expanse of ocean and sends a huge splash along the surface.

"Now you're showing off."

We walk along the pebbled path to a small dock that extends into the ocean. The salt air is mixed with the scent of far-off bonfires, and as we get to the end of the dock, Aero threads his fingers through mine. I try to keep my grin to myself, but it gets away, crawling up my cheeks and sending sparks through my spine.

We get to a small boat that's bobbing softly off the wharf with Aero's name inscribed in green along the side.

Aero turns and shrugs his shoulders, showing off his ridiculous smile again.

A picnic hamper sits on the floor of the boat. "This is far too cute."

"Not bad, huh?" Aero says, hopping onto the boat and giving me his hand to take.

Once we're both settled, Aero takes the oars from their riggers and begins rowing. The sea is calm, and the light that's fading away reflects across the surface like molten lava.

We get about a hundred meters from the dock, and Aero motions his left hand at the oars, like the conductor of a big brass band. They continue to row without him, taking us slowly across the water.

Aero hands me a glass filled with something red and sparkling. "So, you never told me why you moved here."

"Divorce," I say, taking a sip.

"Sorry?"

"Not me," I say with a laugh. "Mum and Dad. They started getting a divorce around the same time I was figuring out my magic, so they figured it'd be a good time for me to learn from Gran."

Aero takes a sip from his own drink. "That's rough."

"Yes and no. I think the hardest part was watching two people fall out of love. That and my own past experiences with relationships, and it kinda… I dunno, I guess it made me lose a lot of confidence in the whole happily-ever-after thing."

Aero looks at the ocean rolling past us and then back at me. "Your own past experiences? So, you *have* been divorced?"

"Nah, just didn't have the greatest ex-boyfriend," I say, turning to look back at the harbor that is slowly glowing to life with lights popping up across all the tiny houses.

Aero sits quietly.

"Sorry, I didn't mean to be a downer," I say.

"No," Aero says, looking over. "I was just thinking: I know what that's like."

I smile. "It's the whole trust thing. I put everything I could into trusting him, and he just shit all over it by running off with someone else. That really messes with—"

"With your heart," Aero finishes for me. "I know."

I sense he wants to say more, but instead, he just looks at me, really looks.

"But I'm glad I'm here," I say, returning his stare. "You seem pretty trustworthy."

Aero smiles before looking at his dusty sneakers and fiddling with his laces.

Nineteen

WHEN I GET HOME FROM my date with Felix, I immediately kick my shoes off and slump on the enormous beanbag in the corner of the room.

This is my happy place. Gran made sure it had everything I needed to feel comfortable while she spent months out of town. My record player sits atop a stack of books next to the TV and a poster of *The Rocky Horror Picture Show* hangs above it. My favorite part is the privacy. Gran lives in the main house out front, but this is my cabin, my sanctuary. I need this after the night I've had.

Felix seemed so innocent earlier, when his big brown eyes confided in me about his past. It meant so much to me, and at the same time, it made me feel like the biggest piece of shit. I know I should've mentioned what I saw, but it's too much. I feel like I really like this guy. Really like him. I don't know what it is that makes me feel like a ten-year-old with a boyband crush, but he just does something to me.

I will tell him. I have to. But right now, I just want him to be safe. I want him to know that it's all going to be OK. He deserves that.

I snuggle into the beanbag, throw a blanket over my legs, and open my phone.

I scroll through my social media feeds and wave an incantation at the kitchen. A glass of cool cranberry juice floats over and lands in my hand.

After some mindless scrolling, I think about Felix and immediately feel warmer, like I've just sunk into a bubble bath. I'm about to open a new message when there's a knock. Gran peeks her head through the front door.

"Hi, love," Gran says, waving with a hand that's dripping with emerald bracelets.

I sit up and force myself off my beanbag, somehow managing not to drop any of my juice.

"Hi, Gran."

"I know that look." Gran closes the door behind her and pulls out a seat at the kitchen table.

I'm constantly in awe at how glamorous she is. She is wrapped in a giant purple velvet coat, and her heels are sharp enough to puncture a tire.

"What look?" I ask. I take a seat next to her and fiddle with the tablecloth, trying to avoid eye contact.

"That doe-eyed, can't-stop-thinking-about-someone look," Gran says with a smirk. "How was your date?"

I sigh. It's near impossible to keep anything from her, but to be honest, it's kind of cute she cares. "It was... Yeah."

"It was *yeah*? What on earth does *yeah* mean?" Gran snaps her fingers and manifests two mugs of hot chocolate out of thin air.

"Special," I say, taking a sip of the deliciously sweet drink and looking into the swirling milkiness.

"Well, well, well. Special is a pretty great *yeah*, I must say."

I shrug. "I dunno. He's a good one, you know? I want to do right by him."

Gran nods, leans in close, and pats my knuckles. "Just be you, and he'll be putty in your hands."

I smile. The last thing I want is for him to be "putty," but the reassurance is nice.

"Noted," I say, taking another sip.

Gran swirls her finger around the rim of her mug. "I just wanted to let you know I'll be out of town for the next couple of days. The girls are looking after the shop, but I'd love it if you could keep an eye on them while I'm gone."

I nod. "Of course. Where are you off to this time?" I ask.

"I'm going to do some investigating." Gran bounces her eyebrows up and down.

"Investigating?"

"Indeed. You don't think I'm just going to sit around idly while people keep going missing, do you?"

Gran is like a bulldog with a chew toy when she focuses on something. Normally, I'd be impressed, but the thought of her digging into stuff and uncovering Felix's gran makes me feel cold. This whole situation is a real mess, and I can already feel a headache coming on.

"Be careful," I say, looking anywhere but at her.

"Darling, is something wrong? Something you want to talk about?"

I keep my eyes on the window and shake my head. "Nope, I'm good."

Gran sits with me for a moment before taking a final sip of her hot chocolate, standing, and giving me a kiss on the head. "See you soon." She turns on her beautiful bloodred heels and heads outside.

Twenty

THERE ARE FEW TIMES IN my life when I have been literally speechless, like the time I backed into a garbage truck during my driving test, or the time I fell off the stage at school when I was in a production of *Oliver!*

Today is another scenario entirely. That night with Aero was the most ridiculously cute date I have ever been on, and I have an army of butterflies having an all-out war in my tummy.

When I get home, Gran is already asleep in bed, and Newt is curled in a ball on my pillow.

"Hey, cutie," I say, rubbing Newt's giant ears and coaxing him to the end of my bed so I can get in.

I kick off my shoes and get down to just my undies and T-shirt before taking a deep breath in and staring up at the ceiling.

I feel like I'm resisting being happy about this. Being happy would mean lowering my guard, becoming vulnerable, and opening up the possibility of full-blown heartbreak later down the track.

No thank you.

I close my eyes and try to remember a spell I saw in *Incantations, Herbs & Astrology*.

Newt is already back to snoring, so when I clap my hands four times and focus them on the ceiling, he jumps like the house has been hit by lightning.

The ceiling fizzles and fades, and the night sky above replaces my view. I have to admit, I'm stoked I pulled that off on the first go.

I give Newt a scratch on his belly and lay back down to stare at the sky. The pitch darkness is sprinkled with thousands upon thousands of tiny flecks of light, and I do my best to count as many as I can.

I'm up to forty-nine when my phone buzzes and illuminates the room.

Fern has created a group message with me, Aero, and Charlie.

Fern: We NEED to talk. Like ASAP!

I squeeze my eyes shut before typing back.

Felix: Crock Pot? Tomorrow morning?

I've barely hit send before Fern confirms.

When I get to the Crock Pot, the others are already inside, enjoying hot chocolates in a booth and speaking under their breath.

"Hey," I say, scooting in next to Aero, who gives a squeeze on my thigh and smiles that ridiculous smile of his.

"OK," Fern says. She takes a deep breath. "I found something."

Fern puts a dusty tome in the center of the table, the paper frayed and yellowed. The cover has a simple circle of faded gold in the middle and no mention of an author.

Aero looks over to me and shrugs.

Charlie leans in for a closer look. "What *is* this exactly?"

"I visited Granddad Tompkin at the library last night when he was closing up and discovered this." Fern opens the book and finds a page with REVEALION SPELL written in swirly script across the top of the page.

"It's an old spell that was used back when covens were much more in demand. If a witch was considered to be using her powers for evil, the coven would order a Revealion Spell to have the truth told."

Aero glances at me and back at the book. His face lights up. "Umm, this is awesome. So all we need to do is perform the spell, and whoever is doing this will reveal themselves... Right?"

Fern nods slowly, taking everything in. "Correct, but it's not as simple as that."

"Of course, it isn't," Charlie says, rolling his eyes.

"We need some essentials," Fern says, turning the page and pointing down a list.

Revealion Spell

Ingredients

1. Hair of mermaid
2. Dragon scale
3. Eye of newt
4. Mugwort
5. Lavender
6. Poppy seeds

Method:

Brew cauldron with lamb's milk and add ingredients throughout while chanting: Ipsum revelare.

When the milk has turned lilac, the spell will be complete.

I take a deep breath.

"So, nice and easy then?" I say with a short laugh.

"*Mermaid hair?*" Aero exclaims, looking up at Fern.

"*That's* what you're worried about?" Charlie says, his face losing color with every word. "You don't think dragon scales are slightly more terrifying?"

"OK, just… Let's take a beat to think," Fern says, looking between the three of us. "We are perfectly capable of getting these ingredients together. Aero, you've been a pro for as long as I can remember, and Felix, you're getting stronger by the day."

Charlie looks up, waiting for an acknowledgment.

"And, of course, Charlie is more than able to—"

"Are we sure about this?" I say, my voice croaky.

The table goes quiet for a moment as we let this all sink in.

Aero looks at me and says, "I'm in."

"Me too," Fern says.

"And me," Charlie says, quieter than the others.

I close the book. "OK. Let's get started."

Twenty-One

When I get home, Gran is out in the backyard picking chocolate fudge from her garden and humming an old Sam Cooke tune. Yes, *chocolate fudge from her garden*. I thought I'd be used to this stuff by now, but that just blows my mind. Newt sits patiently next to her, waiting for any stray fudge and licking the air like it's made of peanut butter.

"There you are, darling," Gran says, putting her basket down and bundling me up in a hug.

"Hey." I breathe in her perfume and smile as Newt makes a dash for the fudge basket.

"Nice try, doofus." Gran leads Newt's giant head away. "Now, how are you?"

I look anywhere but at her, my heart doing a weird backflip that makes me feel like I'm on the Waltz ride at the local fair.

"We, uhh," I start, trying to form a sentence in my mind, "found out some stuff."

Gran stands taller, her eyes searching for mine. "Some stuff?"

I nod. "We think we might be able to figure out what's going on in town."

I let the words sit between us.

Gran picks up her blackberry basket and leads me inside.

When we get to the kitchen, Gran gives me a peck on the head and rearranges the cupboards with a wave of her hand, baking mixture toppling out of boxes and chocolate fudge pieces whizzing through the air.

"W-What?" I say, ducking as three stray eggs whoosh past my ear.

"An adventure requires strength, and there's no better strength to be found than within my double choc fudge brownies."

I laugh as Gran continues to send ingredients flying.

Newt wiggles his butt and leaps, attempting to grab whatever ingredients he can.

When at last the brownies are safely in the oven, Gran pulls up a kitchen stool next to me and pats my arm. "I have just one request, my darling." Her is voice softer and more serious than I've heard it in a while. "I need you to be careful not to fall in love."

I scoff and laugh at once, which produces a quacking sound. "OK, Gran. Firstly, that is highly doubtful, with my current insecurities and major avoidance to anything resembling love. Secondly, are you sure it's just chocolate in those brownies? You're sounding odd…"

Gran shakes her head and stares at me for a moment. "You're getting far too old. I just, there's something—"

Three knocks on the front door cut Gran off mid-sentence.

"I'll get it," I say, making my way toward the hall and checking the peephole.

Demelza is standing on the front porch. She's wearing a red velvet dress with her hair tied in a messy bun atop her head.

When I open the door, Demelza winks like she knew it would be me to open it.

"Hey," I say, giving her a hug.

"You get more handsome every time I see you, Spud," Demelza says. She's caught on to Gran's nickname for me.

Gran wipes flour from her forehead onto her skirt. "Demelza! Just the person I wanted to see."

"What can I say? I know when I'm needed," Demelza says with a grin, following Gran into the kitchen.

Somehow the brownies are already ready and displayed on a cake tray, a sprinkle of icing sugar across their surface to highlight the gooey chocolate chunks throughout.

I pull up a stool. "OK, they look *a-mazing*."

"Psh-psh," Gran says, waving away my hands. "Now, Demelza, while I've got you, I need you to put a charm on these ridiculously delicious brownies for me."

Demelza chuckles to herself, inspecting the plate of brownies. "And what charm exactly will you be requiring exactly, Aggie?"

Gran looks over at me briefly. "Protection. Bundles of it."

"Gran, I haven't even told you where I'm—"

"As if you needed to *tell me*." Gran says, rolling her eyes. "Now, Demelza, if you please."

Demelza looks to me and smiles softly, adjusting the obsidian ring on her pinky finger. Her hands hover above the brownies. "Praesidium, quod amor lucis."

At first, I think nothing is happening. The only sound is coming from the clock above the oven.

Then, without warning, Demelza's hands literally set alight.

"HOLY SH—"

Gran grabs my arm. Apparently, even when someone is literally on fire, I'm not allowed to swear.

Purple and blue flames lick across Demelza's arms and through her fingers, engulfing the brownies yet somehow not burning them to a cinder.

Eventually the flames flicker out, and the brownies look just as they did before.

I look between Gran and Demelza, slowly shaking my head and trying to focus on my breathing.

"Th-That's some pretty, uh… impressive pyrotechnics," I say, my mouth void of saliva.

Demelza chuckles and does a curtsy.

"Not bad for an old broad," Gran says with a wink.

"I came to discuss—" Demelza starts.

"Yes yes yes. And discuss we shall. But let's wait until Felix is sorted for his adventure."

I look between them both, aware they're not saying anything.

"Now is a good a time as any," Gran says, looking at me and smiling. "Just one moment."

Gran leaves Demelza and me silently standing in the kitchen.

When she returns, she's holding a wooden box the size of a cigar tin. A simple S is engraved across the top in silver ink.

"For you," Gran says, handing me the box.

Demelza gives me a smile as I look down at the polished wood.

I slowly pull the clasp around the divide and open the box to reveal a small silver teaspoon with a tiger's eye stone nestled in the tip.

"Gran, th-thank you."

The teaspoon emits a soft glow and vibrates through the box.

"You're as ready as you'll ever be, my darling," Gran says, pecking me on the top of the head. "Now, be careful."

I nod and walk toward the stairs before turning back and giving her an all-encompassing hug.

"I love you," I say, squeezing her tight. "See you soon, Demelza."

Gran strokes my arm. "I love you too, my special boy."

I head upstairs to my room and pull out my duffel bag from my wardrobe.

Before grabbing my copy of *Incantations, Herbs & Astrology* and my new teaspoon, I stuff a change of clothes, deodorant, my toothbrush, and a pack of mints into the bag. Because my priority is a cute guy I'm kind of infatuated with.

I turn the teaspoon over in the palm of my hand and feel a hum run through my arms. Gran seemed onboard, even without knowing what the hell I'm about to do. I should be really stoked, but I have a nagging feeling she knows more than she's letting on.

My phone vibrates.

Fern: Meet at the White Horse at 7?

That's half an hour away. Time for me to give myself a once-over in the mirror and douse myself in cologne. I don't know why, but ever since the night on the boat with Aero, I've become painfully self-conscious.

I type back a thumbs-up emoji.

WHEN I GET TO THE White Horse, the smell of stale beer and dusty floorboards is somewhat comforting. I shut the creaky wooden door behind me and find myself a table near the back.

The seats are upholstered in scratchy paisley fabric with a few rock-hard patches where drinks have spilled.

I throw my duffel bag under the table and sit on my leg to stop it from jackhammering the floor.

Fern is the first to arrive, followed by Charlie. They both throw their bags underneath the table and sit in front of me, leaving the seat next to me open for Aero. I'm pretty sure we're all on the same page when it comes to whatever is (or isn't) going on with me and Aero.

Charlie is fidgeting more than usual, but Fern seems completely calm and businesslike.

Fern pulls her backpack out from under the table and opens it. "Aero is just picking up a few things from home, and then we can go over everything, but I figured we might as well start as close to home as possible."

I nod. Charlie doesn't blink.

"Just off the coast of Dorset Harbor are the Cornall Caves." Fern takes out a small map from inside her bag and places it on the table. "Sailors have been warned to avoid the caves for centuries because it's mermaid territory. They can be a little—"

"Deadly," Charlie chimes in, still unblinking.

"OK, chill out," Fern says, rolling her eyes. "First of all, they're just territorial. If we can get there at night while they rest, it should be easy."

"Should be," I say, more to myself than to them. "So, where are these caves then?"

"Right about—"

"There," Aero says, as if appearing out of nowhere and tapping a point on the map with his index finger.

"Hey," I say, smiling up at him.

He's wearing a sherpa jacket over a flannel shirt and some black jeans. He looks ridiculously attractive right now.

"Hi, you," he says, squeezing in next to me and placing his hand on my thigh.

A million bolts of electricity run through my body. That simple touch sends my heart into the stratosphere.

Fern looks between both of us and giggles to herself. She flicks her finger to point between us. "If this weren't such an important mission, you two would actually be *very* cute right now."

I grin as Aero gives my thigh another rub.

"Back to the plan," Charlie says. Do his eyes have any moisture left at all, or have they just dried open permanently?

"Of course," Aero says. "The plan! Well, to get to the Cornall Caves, we'll need a boat." He throws a set of keys onto the table and leans back, a giant grin on his face.

"Perfect," Fern says, giving Charlie a nudge. "You OK there, Charlie?"

He blinks for the first time, which is a relief. It was starting to freak me out.

"Y-Yeah. Yeah, fine. Just," he looks down at the table for a moment, gathering his thoughts. "I guess I'm just worried my magic isn't... well, up to par with you guys..."

Fern places a hand on Charlie's and gives it a stroke. "You have *nothing* to worry about, OK? You are more talented than you give yourself credit for, and you need to start believing in yourself."

"I agree," Aero says.

"Me too," I add.

Charlie's shoulders release some tension, and the hint of a smile crosses his lips.

"There's no time to waste," Fern says, addressing all of us. "I say we get going tonight."

Aero nods, and Charlie does too.

We all order sausage and mash with Yorkshire puddings and thick gravy as we slowly go over the route on the map.

Charlie's fears linger in the back of my mind. What if he *isn't* OK out there? I mean, my magic isn't amazing, but I know how to do enough to keep my head above water. I don't know if I'll be up for looking after him too.

After we've sopped up the gravy with our Yorkshire puddings and finished our drinks, we head out into the cool evening air.

When we get to the dock, the stars are like a thousand pinpricks in a black canvas. The only sounds comes from the lapping of water against the dock and the occasional bullfrog or seagull nearby.

"It's nothing fancy," Aero says, hopping into his small boat and putting his bag under one of the seats. "But it'll get us there."

Fern looks paler than before, a hint of uncertainty on her face as she slowly steps into the boat.

"As the famous Chief Brody once said: 'We're gonna need a bigger boat,'" Charlie says, shaking his head.

"Charlie, come on. We'll be absolutely fi—"

"Fern, please. Just be real with me for a second. You *know* what mermaids are capable of. They'll tip this thing the moment they see it."

I decide not to contribute. I have no idea what mermaids are capable of, and if Charlie's right, then we're taking one hell of a gamble.

"Listen, it's past eleven. The resting hours have begun. If we keep steady and make as little noise as possible, they'll never know we're there."

"Do I need to remind you what we need from the mermaid? Forgive me for thinking that it's going to be difficult to go unnoticed while we give her a haircut."

"Charlie, if you'd rather stay, we'll understand," Aero says gently. "But at this point, it's our only option."

Charlie leans from foot to foot, the tension in his shoulders building up again. "N-No, I'm coming," he finally says, shaking his head as he gets into the boat.

I'm the last in, and I put my teaspoon in my pocket as I stow my backpack underneath the seat next to Aero's.

"Ahoy," Aero says as he pulls the engine cord and the boat rumbles to life.

Fern places two hands on the engine and says, "*Quiescic.*" A faint gold glow radiates around the motor as it quiets down to nothing more than a whisper.

Aero then taps the top twice and takes a seat next to me, placing his hand on my thigh again and smiling.

"Cruise control," he says as we continue puttering out into the black, velvety ocean.

Twenty-Two

CHARLIE HAS BARELY SAID TWO words since we set off from the dock, and Fern looks like she could be getting whiplash from the constant craning of her neck over the side of the boat. I haven't taken my hand off Felix and, thankfully, he seems to be comfortable with it.

We're farther out than I've ever been before, the little dotted coastline barely visible now that we're out on the blue ocean.

I give Felix's thigh a squeeze before standing and heading toward the motor of the boat, patting Charlie on the shoulder as I go to assure him that everything's OK and we're not about to sink.

I pull my backpack from under the seat and retrieve the map Fern brought along. We're getting closer to the Cornall Caves, and I feel my lunch churning in my stomach.

I need to stop overthinking—the whole situation with Felix is making my head hurt. I figure if we cast the spell and reveal that Aggie has played a part in all this, he won't take it nearly as hard as if I were to tell him I saw her out in the forest. The fact is, I didn't see Aggie doing anything but standing near the girl. That's not reason enough for him to believe that she was up to no good. I know it's not the brightest move, to keep something from him, but I can't see him hurt. I'm really starting to feel things for him, and that scares me almost as much as the mermaids.

We keep puttering along until the faintest outline of cliffs come into view.

Fern looks back at me and nods, and Felix smiles briefly before giving Charlie a thumbs-up, which he gives back half-heartedly.

We round the outskirts of the cliffs, and I spot the first sight of the Cornall Caves as they come into view.

The rocks around the entrance are jagged and mossy with thousands of oyster shells and crustaceans poking off the surface.

Fern holds her hand in front of the engine, which slows it to a stop, and we sit bobbing in the waves for a moment to gather ourselves.

"OK," I say, looking between the three of them.

Charlie's knee has a mind of its own and is bouncing up and down, like he's actively trying to kick a hole through the bottom of the boat.

"Charlie, mate, you're going to have to take some breaths, yeah?" I say, patting him again as I pull Felix's backpack out from under the seat and hand it to him.

Felix hands Charlie a small paper-wrapped parcel. "Here, take this."

"W-What is it?" Charlie asks, turning the parcel over in the palm of his hand.

"Gran made it. It'll calm you… I think?" Felix says with a shrug.

My thoughts instantly go to Aggie, and I hate myself for thinking the worst.

Charlie opens the paper and reveals a small chocolate brownie from within.

"Got any more of those?" I ask, figuring there is no way Aggie would put her own grandson in any kind of danger. Whatever is going on with her, I *know* she wouldn't do that.

Charlie finishes off his brownie in two bites.

"Yeah, I'd be up for one," Fern says.

Felix hands each of us a similar wrapped package, and Fern and I each take a bite. The chocolate gooey chunks are the first thing I notice. It's probably the best damn brownie I've ever eaten, and I'm not ashamed to say it.

Within five minutes, I feel the first flicker of anxiety leaving my body. It's almost like watching the sun drift behind a cloud: you know it's still there, but the cloud gives you a break from the rays.

Fern looks around, like she's seeing the ocean in all its glory for the first time. The tension in her shoulders from a moment before eases, and she sits up taller, more businesslike than usual—quite an achievement for Fern, considering she's already the one who always has it all together.

"OK, so our plan," Fern says, looking at me and clapping her hands together.

Charlie stands, hands on his hips and surveying the landscape like a safari guide.

"We're going to need bait," Charlie says.

Felix looks to me with raised eyebrows, and I can't quite figure out what Charlie is on about.

"Um… bait?" I say, taking a seat next to Fern.

"Mermaids take sailors and fisherman by luring them in with their songs. We need someone to be lured and someone to be ready to get the hair."

Felix takes a slow, deep breath in, and Fern seems to be calculating it all the possible outcomes in her head.

"OK," Fern says, looking between the three of us.

"I'll—" I start, but Charlie cuts me off.

"I'll do it," he says, nodding like the matter is settled.

Felix wipes a crumb of brownie from the corner of his mouth and looks up at me, his beautiful big eyes searching my face for some reassurance that it's all going to be OK.

Fern hovers her hand above the engine, and it spurts to life, silently sending us toward the cave.

Twenty-Three

OK, SO GRAN'S BROWNIES ARE next level. I knew whatever she was making would help with our journey, but hearing Charlie volunteer to be bait for a mermaid when only twenty minutes ago, he was going to have a full-blown panic attack makes me think Gran has some serious power.

The Cornall Caves are enormous and intimidating as we make our way toward them. The water is gray, and the closer we get to the entrance, the more the swell of the ocean throws us around.

Aero comes and sits next to me, putting an arm around my waist and kissing my shoulder. I don't know when this kind of public display of affection began, but I am more than happy about it. I've never been with anyone who went out of their way to show me they care with the simple act of holding my hand or wrapping me in a hug in the middle of a busy street. It's weirdly comforting. I guess this must be what it feels like to be straight. To never second-guess showing who you're with that you care, to not be in fear of someone abusing you for being yourself.

Fern looks over at us and smiles, and Charlie is looking in all directions, like he's the captain.

Charlie pushes the mop of hair from his eyes and adjusts his glasses. "We're getting close."

Aero stands and joins Charlie as Fern waves her palm and cuts the engine, letting us slowly pass through the entrance and into the dark of the caves.

It takes a moment for my eyes to adjust, but soon enough, they can make out the long, sharp teeth of the caves' roof and the flickering glowworms that line the mossy rocks above and below.

The water inside the cave becomes still, and our boat drifts for a moment, keeping its distance from the rocks and sharp barnacles.

I'm about to speak when I first hear it. Soft, almost angelic tones whisper along the caves' ceiling from somewhere deep below. It's a language I can't understand, not so much words as it is a melody of strung-out letters, each individually more haunting than the last.

I wonder if anyone else can hear it when Aero lifts his hands and motions for all of us to stay still.

Charlie gives Aero a thumbs-up and then looks to me and Fern with an expression that isn't as confident as he was after eating the brownie.

He then gets on his knees, holds the side of the boat, and peers into the deep blue ocean beneath us.

Aero slowly makes his way to sit next to me, and Fern and I each retrieve a pair of scissors from within our backpacks.

The sound seems to be getting louder, but I can't tell if it's just the echo of the cave or if there's more than one.

Charlie looks back at us as a splash from somewhere behind

makes the boat rock, forcing Aero to grab hold of the side to avoid toppling in.

"Charlie," I say, helping Aero sit, "what now?"

"It's OK," Charlie says, steadying himself in the center of the boat and craning his neck to listen. "D-Do you have any more of that brownie?"

I dig out another piece from my bag and pass it to him. He inhales it, like he hasn't eaten in days, as another splash, closer this time, makes all of us jump.

"OK, maybe this wasn't such a—" Fern starts as another splash, even closer, makes her stop mid-sentence.

Charlie kneels along the side of the boat, spotting something below the surface.

I look to Aero, who has the same confused look on his face as Fern.

"Charlie?" I whisper.

The water around the boat ripples gently, the last of the splashing drifting off and the water returning to calm.

"It's OK..." Charlie says. "I think they're—"

An eruption of water engulfs Charlie from where he's standing, knocking Fern, Aero, and me to the bottom of the boat as a long, slick hand grabs Charlie by the throat, pulling him overboard and into the murky water.

"NO!" Fern screams, scrambling to the side of the boat and grabbing at nothing as Charlie is pulled farther and farther under.

Aero flings his arm at the ocean and yells, "*Gurgitem Abripuit!*"

The water sloshes and turns over, like bathwater gurgling down a sinkhole.

We're thrown every which way as our boat churns across the enormous swell the whirlpool is creating.

"WHAT ARE YOU DOING?" I scream over the top of the roaring water.

Our boat continues to thrash across the enormous waves as the whirlpool keeps up its spiral to the bottom of the sea.

"AERO, I SEE HIM!" Fern shouts, pointing over the side of the boat into the darkness below.

Charlie is twisting and turning under the ocean, grabbing at nothing as the long, ghostly mermaid drags him farther down.

I feel sick. My head is spinning, and I can't form a single logical thought.

Aero jumps across a seat next to me and grabs onto the side, peering over to get a glimpse of Charlie.

The whirlpool is keeping the mermaid struggling, but she's strong, and Charlie only has so much breath he can hold.

I scramble underneath the seat for my backpack, throw it open, and rummage through it. I grab my teaspoon from its box and can sense I'm becoming stronger. Aero looks over at me, and I see a glint of a smile in his eyes.

Fern sees what I'm doing and pulls out her own teaspoon as she grabs hold of the side of the boat to lift herself up to stand. With a pointed finger toward the roaring water below, Fern closes her eyes and breathes.

A rush pulses through me. I know what I have to do.

"*INPULSA!*" Fern and I scream together, sending acid-green light waves from the tips of our teaspoons that curl through the bubbling water.

Aero mouths the words *Oh my god* as the water flashes with white and green light, stunning everything into stillness.

The mermaid spasms just once before going limp, her grip on Charlie loosening as they both float stunned beneath us.

"NOW!" Fern bellows, lifting the tip of her teaspoon up and instructing me to do the same.

The whirlpool flashes and erupts all around us as Charlie and the mermaid are pulled back toward the boat.

When Charlie is close enough, Fern and I put away our teaspoons and grab him by the shoulders, pulling his saturated body into the boat.

The mermaid floats silently in the water next to us, and Aero wastes no time. He grabs the scissors from the bottom of the boat and plunges his hand into the water, cutting a chunk of her silky silver hair and pulling it out of the water.

With his other hand, Aero waves violently toward the back of the cave, sending the mermaid into the darkest recesses of the murky water as the whirlpool calms to nothingness.

We collapse in a pile on the bottom of the boat. Charlie heaves and splutters up gallons of salty water, and Aero, Fern, and I breathe like we've been in a house fire.

"I… can't… believe…" Aero starts, holding his hand to his chest. "That… you…"

"Got dragged into the ocean by a mermaid and nearly died?" Charlie says, panting. "Yeah, me neither."

Fern looks across at Charlie and smiles, patting him softly on his chest.

"You got it," I say, noticing the translucent hair still in Aero's grasp.

He smiles at me, and all the blood rushes back to my head at once.

"I did," he says. "Thanks to you lot."

Aero unzips his backpack and takes out a mason jar, which he uses to gather the mermaid hair before screwing on the lid and placing it back inside. He sits up and looks around at the glowworms in the mossy rocks that have started shining again now that the commotion is over. "Let's get the hell out of here."

Fern clicks her fingers and the boat roars to life, taking our bruised and battered bodies back toward home.

Twenty-Four

WHEN WE GET TO THE shore, I can't wipe the smile off my face. Seeing Felix kick ass with Fern back in the Cornall Caves has given me butterflies for days, and I can't stop looking at him. I know it's new, and I know he has a past, but I'm really feeling things for this guy. It's killing me that I haven't spoken to him about Aggie, but I just want to enjoy him right now. No complications. Just us.

We dock the boat and grab our things before clambering onto the wharf and heading for town.

The sun is just starting to rise, and a few seagulls circle us as we make our way up the hill toward the town square. My whole body feels like it's been put in a washing machine, and I'm more exhausted than I've ever been, yet I still feel buzzed and alive. *We did it! We actually got one of the ingredients to cast our spell.*

Fern and Charlie walk up ahead, talking quietly to one another, and Felix walks next to me, his legs trudging up the cobblestone hill. Every step looks like a challenge to him.

I see his hand by his side and take it in mine. He looks over at me, and I see a flicker of hesitation before a warm smile spreads from ear to ear.

"You did so good today…" I say, giving his hand a little squeeze.

He squeezes back. "You did too."

We eventually get to the Crock Pot and slump ourselves in a booth. The place is practically empty; the only other patrons are a couple of sailors enjoying their cups of black coffee near the counter.

Isla pops her head around the corner in the kitchen and winks at me before grabbing a notepad and heading to our booth. "Early one this morning, gang!" She takes her pencil from behind her ear and poises it by her notepad for our orders.

Felix gives Isla one of his best smiles, and I practically melt into my seat.

"A pot of your strongest coffee and four cups, please, Isla," I say.

Isla gives a thumbs-up. "Coming right up."

Fern crosses her arms on the table in front of her and rests her head. Charlie looks like he could sleep for a year—after showering, obviously. He's still damp, the seat squeaking whenever he moves.

I open my backpack to check that the mason jar is still safe and take a second to look at the otherworldly hair glowing from within.

"We did it," I say, patting Felix's knee under the table.

Fern lifts her head weakly and smiles. "We did."

Isla comes back with a large pot of coffee and four big mugs. "Another one went missing last night." She shakes her head. "Dropping like flies."

All of us turn to her like we've been given a shot of adrenaline.

"Patrick Eaves..." Isla says, looking down at her shoes.

"Did anybody see anything?" Fern asks.

Isla shakes her head. "If this doesn't get sorted soon, I'll be shipping my young'uns off to boarding school. I'm barely sleeping."

Fern, Felix, Charlie, and I all look between each other as Isla heads back to the kitchen.

I turn to Felix and open my mouth, the thought of telling him about Aggie balancing on the tip of my tongue.

"We need to move fast," Charlie says, adjusting his glasses.

"What's next?" Fern asks, taking out a piece of paper with the ingredients from within her bag and placing it on the table in front of us.

We all peer over the crumpled paper to read:

Dragon scale.

Twenty-Five

IT'S ASTONISHING HOW WEIRD LIFE is sometimes.

For example, just a few months ago, I was living with Mum and Dad in our house in Oakington, I went to a regular school, occasionally went for a run, and I would confidently say the most exciting part of my week was when Mum made her famous chicken risotto.

Cut to now, and it's ridiculous that I'm trying to figure out where the hell we'll find a *dragon scale*.

When I get home, Gran is nowhere to be seen. Newt, on first look, appears to be re-landscaping the backyard. It's only when I get closer that I realize he's digging up an old bone, then replanting it elsewhere—I'm thinking it's because he saw me watching him.

I give Newt a pat on his giant head, somehow avoiding the mounds of dirt he's kicking up, and head inside.

The house seems quieter than normal. The kitchen doesn't look like anyone's been in there for a while, and the living room is tidy, almost unlived in. Not a single stray cookie crumb or empty teacup is to be found.

Upstairs, my bed is made, and the room smells like cinnamon. A small brown parcel sits atop my bedside drawer, wrapped in string with a piece of a card attached.

I think you'll be needing these. X is scrawled in Gran's perfect handwriting across the card.

I take the brown parcel and sit on my bed as Newt peers his head around the door.

"Hey, cutie," I say, patting the bed to invite him up.

He bounds over, taking out everything in his path with his giant tail and making himself comfy next to me, then burrowing his head into my side.

I give Newt a scratch before slowly untying the string that wraps the parcel. Through the brown paper wrapping is another pouch, tied with string almost as translucent as the mermaid hair. It's heavy. Heavier than something this size ought to be. I pull at the drawstring and let the contents pool out onto the bed next to me.

It takes me a second to figure out what I'm looking at. Gloves. Not ordinary winter gloves that are fluffy and cozy and inspire cups of tea and fireplaces. This is some serious, chain-link, silver badassery.

I turn them over in my hands before slipping my left hand in to one of them. I can't get over how heavy they are as I try to lift my left over to help put my right in.

When both gloves are on, I flip my hands a few times to get a proper feel. I have to admit, I feel pretty awesome.

I lean over to my bedside drawer and grab my phone, but there's no way in hell I'm going to be able to unlock the screen with these metal fingers. So I focus my power and float my phone in front of me, my camera levitating midair, and open the camera app to snap a photo of me in all my medieval glory.

I watch as my phone opens a message to Aero, attaches the photo, and sends it on its way.

Newt pokes his head out from under the mound of sheets he's burrowed himself in and sniffs at the chain-link gloves.

"Pretty awesome, huh?" I say, watching the light reflect off the gray metal as Newt gets comfy again.

I slowly take them off and put them back in their pouch when my thoughts drift to Gran. How did she know we needed a dragon scale?

I try not to think too much into it and shrug it off as just another bizarre thing that continually keeps happening when my phone vibrates.

Aero: OK, I was attracted to you before. What are you doing to me?

I grin.

Felix: Just preparing to slay a dragon...

I kick off both my shoes and lay back on my bed.

Aero: You are most certainly slaying...

I'm blushing.

The weirdest thing about this whole situation is we've literally only been on one kinda-sorta date. I don't know why, but I feel so much closer to him than I expected. I'm sure the whole battling-a-mermaid thing played a part in that, but still.

I turn over and check the clock next to my bed: 7:48 AM. I've been awake for over a day, and it's a struggle to keep my eyes open.

Newt kicks a leg out, and I rearrange my pillows so the both of us are comfy before closing my eyes and drifting off to sleep.

AT FIRST I THINK I'M dreaming. It's only when Newt barks a fourth time that my eyes ping open and I realize I'm awake.

"NEWT!" I shout, jumping out of bed and running downstairs to find him.

The house is still empty, and upon checking the clock by the front door, I realize it's nearly six o'clock at night. Gran should be home.

The house is cold and holds that same quiet, eerie feeling I felt before.

I follow the sound of Newt's roaring barks until I find him standing at the double doors in the living room, looking out toward the backyard.

"HEY!" I shout as Newt jumps on one of the couches to get a better look outside. "What the hell has gotten into…"

My skin goes cold as my eyes adjust.

Is it a shadow?

That's when I see it.

Just a few steps from the double doors stands the strangest creature I've ever seen.

Its eyes are small pinpricks of red that cut through the night like a demon.

The thin creature stands staring, it's ears pointing to the stars.

I open my mouth to say something, but nothing comes out.

I swallow twice. "Newt…" I whisper, barely breathing. "Newt, get upstairs."

Newt's ears pin to his head, and for the first time ever, he listens to me, turns, and races up the stairs to my room.

I never take my eyes off the creature, who is just standing; the only thing I can make out are the tiny bloodred eyes.

I inch my hand toward my pocket, visualizing my teaspoon on my bedside drawer.

The creature creaks its neck to the right, as if challenging me.

I clutch my teaspoon as the creature makes a sound unlike anything I've ever heard. A piercing roar makes the windows rattle in their frames as I pull my teaspoon out and point.

The blinding light that erupts from my teaspoon knocks me back a few steps. The creature recoils in horror before turning and running into the woods.

The room spins as I sit on the carpet and catch my breath.

When I look up again, the darkness has engulfed the backyard, the creature nowhere to be seen.

Twenty-Six

I WAKE TO THE SOUND of knocking at my door. Well, more like someone is trying to knock the thing off its hinges.

I get out of bed and throw on a singlet, not bothering to look for pants, what with the four horsemen of the apocalypse trying to break my door down and all.

I get to the front door and open it a crack to peek out.

"Felix, wh-what are you—"

Felix barges past me, breathing like he ran the entire way here. He's followed by Newt, who runs to the corner of the room, chases his tail three times, and lies down, clearly spooked.

"S-Sorry, it's just," Felix starts before clocking that I'm still in my underwear and singlet. "Sorry," he says again, a blush creeping across his cheeks.

"It's fine. Sit, what's going on?"

He looks around the room, calming his breathing as he takes everything in. It's by no means anything fancy, but it's got my personality sprinkled throughout it. My old vinyl record player sits next to a poster of *The Goonies*, and I've got incense burning in a wooden sculpture that looks like a cupped hand.

"Some... *thing* was just at my house," Felix says, taking a seat on the couch and directing his eyes to the floor.

"*Thing?*" I ask, taking a seat opposite him on a beanbag.

"I can't explain it." He puts his head in his hands, squeezing his eyes shut. "We have got to get the rest of the ingredients and put an end to this. I'm losing my mind."

I get closer to Felix and pull him into a hug. "Come here."

He smells like lavender and cinnamon, and I want nothing more than to make him feel better. I don't know when I realized I was falling for him, but holding him here is making everything come into focus.

"You're safe now," I say, giving him an extra squeeze. "All of this will be over with soon. I promise."

Felix lifts his eyes to mine and smiles weakly. "Are you? Are we?" He shakes his head.

I think I know what he's asking, but I can't be sure.

"Are we what?" I say, sitting back so I can really look at him.

Felix rubs his eyes and stands. "Sorry, I don't even know what I'm saying."

"Well," I reply, standing too. "I know what *I'm* saying... And..." I take a step toward him. "I'm falling for you."

Felix shakes his head, and my stomach turns over.

"This is difficult," he says, looking at me and taking a breath.

"OK, not the response I was hoping for, but—"

"Not *you*," Felix says. "This! All of this. I wasn't supposed to feel like this again. I've been hurt before."

I smile. I know I shouldn't because what he's saying has a lot of weight to it, but I smile because it's nice knowing he might feel the same.

"Listen," I say, taking another step toward him and taking his hands in mine. "None of this needs to be difficult. None of it."

Felix looks like he might giggle.

"OK, the mermaid hair and the whole dragon scale thing isn't what I'm talking about. That is *definitely* difficult."

He laughs softly to himself.

"But us? Whatever is going on with us? It doesn't need to be," I continue, gently stroking his fingertips. "I really care about you, Felix. I would never hurt you."

This time, he takes a step toward me.

I inhale slowly, taking a moment to look into his beautiful brown eyes.

He kisses me. Slow at first and then harder, his hands exploring my back and hair.

"I'm falling for you too," he says as I take his hand and lead him to my room.

I WAKE TO FELIX STROKING my arm, the sheet that covers us the only fabric around.

I turn and kiss him, first on the lips and then on the head. He looks so damn cute in the morning, it should be a crime.

"I stayed over," Felix says, more to himself than me.

"You did. You know what that means?"

Felix frowns. He looks like he wants to kiss me and make an emergency escape by jumping out my window simultaneously.

"Pancakes," I say, bouncing my eyebrows. "I'm gonna make you my famous blueberry pancakes."

After we've both had a shower, I hand Felix a pair of old sweatpants, a sweater with a dinosaur on the front, and some extra fluffy socks. The weather outside is gray and miserable, and there's a chill in the air I haven't felt in a while. Perfect pancakes and snuggling weather.

In the living room, I light some kindling in the fireplace. The crackle immediately makes me smile as I throw a log on and rub my hands together.

Felix wanders in and sits on the couch. I didn't think it was possible for him to be any more adorable, but this cozy outfit he's wearing makes me melt.

I head to the kitchen and clap my hands once to warm up. I rarely bother using magic for mundane stuff when I'm on my own, but with Felix here, I feel like showing off.

I turn around and catch him looking, an innocent smile creeping across his face.

With a flick of my wrist, the top cupboard opens, and two mugs shoot out and around the room. I'm careful to avoid shattering the mugs on the ceiling or against the side of Felix's head and instead let them gently float midair next to the kettle.

I then hover the kettle, which starts to bubble and spit shortly after.

Felix laughs from behind me. "What are you *doing?*" he asks, putting his chin in his hands like the cutest puppy dog I've ever seen.

"Trying to—" the kettle dips until I focus my magic back on it, and then I lift it back to the sensible height I was going for. "I'm *trying* to impress you," I say, clicking the fingers of my right hand as a teaspoon lifts from the drawer, scoops two spoonfuls of coffee and plops them into our mugs. "Is it working?" I ask as the kettle slowly pours the boiling water into the mugs before finding its place back on the counter.

"Definitely," Felix says, his eyes looking every which way.

I send Felix's mug over to him, carefully avoiding spilling any.

He grabs it by the ceramic handle and brings it to his lips. "Yum." He places the mug on the little milk crate coffee table in front of him.

I take my levitating mug from the air and sit next to him on the couch.

"Do you always dazzle guys like this?" Felix asks, a cheeky grin on his face. "And girls, sorry—"

I nudge him gently. "What for?"

"I feel like I'm being insensitive."

"For correcting yourself about my sexuality? Or for bringing up other people I've dated after I've made you a delicious cup of levitating coffee?"

Felix's eyes grow wide, clearly entering panic-mode.

"Relax," I say, nudging him again before taking a sip of my own coffee. "You worry. Like, a lot."

Felix nods.

I place a hand on his thigh. "For the record, I've only ever dated two people before meeting you. Both relationships were pretty short-lived, and I can tell you honestly that it was nothing like what we have."

Felix smiles and takes another sip of his coffee.

"But," I start, making Felix's eyes dart back open like a possessed meerkat again. "That shouldn't come into it at all. We all have a past. None of that should come into what is *actually* happening right now."

I put my coffee on the milk crate and face him.

"And what's happening right now?" Felix asks innocently.

"Like I said last night, I'm really falling in—"

A knock at the door nearly sends Felix through the roof, like a Looney Tunes character.

Two seconds later, the door creaks open. Wearing a long emerald velvet cape and white gloves, Gran stands smiling at us, her hand in the doorframe, like some old Hollywood movie star.

"Falling in love?" Gran asks with a wink.

Twenty-Seven

UP UNTIL THIS MOMENT, I thought it was just Aero who could make me feel on the verge of a panic attack with just a glance or a simple sentence.

Aero's grandmother is the definition of glamorous. She doesn't have a hair out of place, and her outfit looks like it came off a *Vogue* cover model.

"Gran," Aero says, standing and heading over to her for a hug. "This is Felix."

"Hi, Mrs.—" I start.

"Oh, psh-psh. No need for that nonsense! I'm Blythe," she says. Her smile is bigger than necessary as she leans in to give me a hug.

"N-Nice to meet you," I say. Her perfume smells like flowers. Expensive flowers.

"Oh, Aero, darling, I didn't mean to bother you, but I just had a call from the grandmother of Prince Charming here wondering if I had seen him," Blythe says, a cheeky look in her eye as Newt stands and stares at her, his head cocked to one side.

I'm not sure why she's so cool with me and her grandson having an adult sleepover in his semidetached studio, but the thought of worrying Gran makes me feel awful.

"I'm so sorry, Mrs.... uh... Blythe. I'll give her a call now. S-Something happened last night, and I was... I came here and—"

Blythe shakes her head. "Don't fret, my love. I let her know you were here and that all was well. You have nothing to stress over."

I nod. I don't know how she knew I was here, but I sure as hell don't feel like asking her. "Thanks," I say, looking at Newt, who still hasn't taken his eyes off her.

Now really isn't the time for Newt to behave like a lunatic and tear up the furniture. I try to communicate with him telepathically to beg him to behave when Blythe speaks again.

"So, what are you two love birds up to today then, hmm?"

"Just having a coffee and maybe watching a movie," Aero says, giving me a wink, which, dear god, I hope Blythe didn't see.

"Well, I'll leave you both to it. But darling, I'm heading out of town again tonight for a few days. Shouldn't be too long. I've got one of the girls looking after the shop while I'm gone."

"OK," Aero says.

Blythe gives him a kiss on the cheek and makes her way to the front door before dramatically turning around to face us both again like a silent film star.

"It was glorious to meet you, my dear," Blythe says, looking at me.

"Likewise," I say with my friendliest smile.

Blythe nods once then knocks three times on the front door.

"Kitchen is stocked with goodies so you don't starve while I'm gone," Blythe says, making her exit.

Sure enough, when Aero opens the cupboards and pantry doors, they are filled with cereals, bread, chips, and cookies. The fridge is practically bursting open with cheese, meats, and soda. I don't know how I'll ever get used to this.

"I really should call my gran," I say, taking my phone from my pocket.

"Sounds good." Aero takes out some chips from the pantry and puts them in a bowl. "I'm gonna see if I can do some tricks with Newt, and then afterwards we can watch *How to Train Your Dragon* for inspiration on our next mission!"

I laugh then head into Aero's bedroom and close the door.

I pace for a few moments before dialing.

Gran answers on the first ring. "Darling, I'm so sorry I wasn't home last night. Demelza and I have been—"

"No, I'm sorry," I say, shaking my head. "I should have let you know where I was and what happened but—"

"What *happened*?" Gran asks. "What do you mean?"

I inhale, and the thought of that spindly creature crawls across my memory like a nightmare.

"Something was at the house. I didn't know... I was scared," I say, uselessly trying to form a sentence to capture what happened.

"Look, the main thing is you are OK," Gran says, taking a deep breath.

I let the silence sit between us for a moment before going on.

A cold sweat breaks on my forehead. "Someone else was taken while we were gone."

"Yes," Gran says, her voice distant.

"Gran? Are you OK?"

Newt barks happily outside. I'm guessing Aero's training is going well.

"I'm absolutely fine, darling," Gran says, her voice upbeat again.

"I think we're getting close to putting an end to all of this," I say, a confidence rising in me that I haven't felt before.

"I think you're right," Gran says. I can hear the smile on her face through the phone.

"It's a good thing you have them gloves then, eh?"

Twenty-Eight

FELIX HAS GONE HOME TO pack a bag of essentials, see his gran, and drop off Newt.

I did some reading a few months ago about dragons, and the closest nest to Dorset Harbor is about three hours away. It's not ideal, but then again, none of this is.

I have three missed calls from Fern and a text from Charlie, asking to meet at the library when I check my phone.

It's 7 AM, and, by the look of things, they've been up all night.

I get in the shower, throw on a sweater and some ripped jeans, and head into town, grabbing a bagel that I heat up in my hand (pyro-magic can be dangerous, yes, but it sure comes in handy when you want a delicious bagel and don't have the time to mess around with a toaster).

When I get to the library, a large stone building on the corner overlooking the harbor, I see another MISSING PERSON sign attached to a telephone pole. The guy in the picture has the same eyes as Felix, and my stomach clenches at the thought of anything happening to him. We need to put an end to this. Fast.

I walk up the mossy steps to the entrance, and I'm greeted by Miss Meadow, who appears to have just gotten directions from the receptionist.

"Oh, hello, Aero!" Miss Meadow says, her giant smile making the dull light of the library entrance glow.

"Hey, Miss Meadow," I say. "Looking for a new book?"

"I'm here to meet Aggie! I just don't know where to—"

"Wendy, good lord, puh-*lease* tell me you haven't brought that parrot of yours along. You'll get me thrown out of this place."

Tomkin stands in the doorway leading to the fiction section, his hand on his hip and showing off his usual furrowed brow.

"*Robin* is at home, actually," Miss Meadow says, clearly ruffled. "Ooh, that reminds me. I need to get bread!"

I chuckle to myself. Regardless of what's going on, Miss Meadow always manages to put a smile on my face.

"I s'pose you're here for the meeting too?" Tomkin says, nodding to me.

"Umm… I'm meeting Fern?"

"Indeed you are. We're through here," he says. He beckons both me and Miss Meadow through the double doors, past the fiction section, and all the way to the back of the room to a table surrounded by chairs, all of which are filled with people I know.

For a second, I feel like they're staging some intervention, then I see Felix and Aggie talking quietly to each other at the end of the table and my shoulders relax.

"Grab yourself a seat, mister," Tomkin says as Miss Meadow plops herself down next to Demelza.

Winifred is sitting next to Fern, who is having her ear chewed off about the price of mugwort. Charlie sits nearby, fiddling with a stray piece of cotton in his sweater.

I wander over to Aggie and Felix, then tap him on the shoulder.

"Hey!" he says, his eyes lighting up.

I glance at Aggie, who gives me the warmest smile I've seen in forever. My mind runs a thousand miles an hour trying to decipher what the hell I saw her doing in the woods that night. She *has* to know something, but I'm too scared of screwing everything up to do anything about it.

"OK, now that we're all here," Tomkin says, his accent drawling along the dusty floorboards, "we wanted to discuss what we think needs to happen for this madness to cease."

I look around the room. Everyone seems either terrified or ready to battle.

Fern catches my eye and gives me a small smile as Charlie stops fiddling and focuses on what's going on.

"Now, my granddaughter here and her band of Goonies have been an instrumental part of bringing this insanity to an end. They are in the process of finding ingredients for a Revealeon Spell and, as much as I'd rather they weren't in danger, my friends and I aren't as flexible as we once were."

Aggie shoots him a glare, and Winifred looks ready to thump him.

"What I think Tomkin is trying to say," Aggie says, standing and dusting off her purple and gold skirt, "Is that we're grateful..." She nods to me, Felix, Fern, and Charlie with a wink.

"Now, none of us know exactly what is causing these disappearances. But we have an idea." Aggie looks to Demelza, who also stands, addressing the room.

"Long ago, something similar happened. A dark witch started stealing the youth energy from children in town to keep her soul young." Demelza's piercing eyes study each of us in turn, slowly and methodically, as if trying to get one of us to break.

"The final spell to keep her soul sprightly was to take the soul of a blood relative."

I look to Felix and feel the ground beneath me fall away. My mind isn't taking any of this in fast enough, but all I can think of is Aggie being behind all of this. What if Aggie is waiting to perform the final spell?

"The catch is, the blood relative must be taken by someone," Demelza continues.

Fern looks to me with a confused frown.

"In simpler terms, the blood relative must be in love."

I look over to Tomkin, who is pacing, his hands deep in his tweed pockets. Miss Meadow looks like she could faint at any moment, and Winifred is sitting quietly, contemplating it all.

"What exactly are you suggesting?" Felix says, his beautiful big eyes scanning the room for some clarification.

Demelza takes a moment to breathe, clearly unsure how to go on.

Aggie looks to Felix and then to me. "We're not entirely sure, but we want you to be careful. Not just on this quest for ingredients but also with your hearts."

I take a deep breath. I'm not certain, but it seems like they're directing all of this to me and Felix, which makes me wonder if others have their suspicions about Aggie as well. I just can't understand how Aggie is going along with it, if that's the case.

"OK," Fern says, standing.

I feel like everyone should be standing at this point, what with everyone jumping in with their two cents every few minutes, but I sit quietly, trying to figure everything out.

"I've done some research, and the closest nest is in Girton Falls, near a town called Draton about three hours away," Fern announces.

The group all face Fern, and Charlie nods, clearly proud to be part of the planning of our next quest.

"The dragon," Charlie says, "is nestled in the caves behind the waterfalls about an hour from the town."

"Aren't dragons avoided at all costs?" I ask. "I mean, that seems really close to a town. Why hasn't it wreaked havoc?"

Felix mouths, *I was going to ask that too*, and winks, making me go to jelly inside.

"Dragons are quiet creatures mostly," Fern says, pacing. "The townspeople of Draton have known about it forever, but they keep to themselves, and the dragon does the same. Sort of like a mutual agreement that if they don't bother him, he won't—"

"Burn their town to a cinder? Got it," I say. "So then that leaves us in a tricky situation. How do we get a scale from the dragon without pissing it off and sending it on a fiery tirade into town?"

Charlie loses some color in his cheeks. "Because we'll be putting it to sleep." He fishes for something in the inside pocket of his overcoat. He puts a small jar in the center of the circle. At first, I think it's empty, until I see the first glimmer of light pop from within. "Fireflies."

"I'm sorry, *fireflies*?" I ask, picking up the jar and taking a peek inside.

They're beautiful, and the gold and purple glow they emit makes me a little drowsy, but I have no idea how something as small as this could take down a giant dragon.

"Bewitched fireflies," Charlie continues. "They will give us about half an hour to take one of the dragon's scales." He takes a small book from within his bag and opens it to a bookmarked section with a diagram. The diagram shows the dragon sprawled out like an insect in a science textbook. "This section here is where we will want to take a scale from. Just near the base of the tail. It's where the old scales eventually shed and are usually the most powerful for potions. I'm hoping it won't take much effort."

I laugh unintentionally at that.

"Sorry," I say, shaking my head. "I just… Wow."

Fern takes the mason jar and the book from Charlie and places them back in his bag.

"We should get going tonight. We can't waste any more time," Fern says.

Felix looks to his gran and smiles, and I immediately wish my gran was here. I haven't told her anything about the Revealeon Spell, and I know how proud she'll be of us. I take comfort knowing Felix has his gran to keep him grounded right now. Hopefully, some of that will rub off on me.

"Sounds like a plan," I say.

Aggie looks over to me. "Be careful, all of you. But especially you two."

The room goes still, and all eyes dart between Felix and me and for the first time since all of this began, I have no idea what to think.

Twenty-Nine

THE WHITE HORSE PUB SEEMS to be our pre-adventure meeting place, and I'm OK with that. They do a mean Yorkshire pudding, and the gravy is so thick, it's like custard.

I check my phone a couple of times to make sure there aren't any last-minute messages calling the whole thing off when the front door opens and Aero walks in, a duffel slung over his shoulder and his hair dripping wet from the storm outside.

We haven't spoken much about the whole sleepover thing, and to be honest, whatever is going on between us is making me really happy. I don't want to go and wreck it by making my feelings, fears, and insecurities get in the way.

Aero stows his duffel under the table and scoots in next to me. "Hey."

He gives me a kiss, and my entire being comes alive. I could kiss him forever and never get bored.

"How are you feeling?" I ask.

"Wet," Aero says with a grin. "But good. I just… I dunno, that whole thing Aggie was talking about left me feeling a little—"

"Confused?" I offer, taking a sip of my lemon, lime, and bitters.

"It's not that I don't understand why they'd be concerned, but what they're insinuating kind of makes me uneasy."

"Yeah," I say, tapping my fingers on the table and trying to think of something useful to say.

"Look, the sooner we get that dragon scale, the sooner we can put an end to all of this and just enjoy whatever this is," I say, motioning between the two of us.

"Whatever *this* is?" Aero says with a wry smile.

I can't stop looking at his eyes. One brown and one green. They're mesmerizing.

"I'd like to think that *this*," Aero says, imitating me and my motioning, "is something pretty cool."

I smile. "Me too." I give him a nudge with my shoulder and put my hand on his thigh.

"I didn't know how else to bring this up but… I'd really like you to be my boyfriend."

A spark runs through me, from my toenails to the top of my head. Hearing those words rocks me to my core. I've never had anyone be so overtly open with their feelings, and as much as I love it, it's also unnerving.

"I'd," I start, my mouth dry and my heart hammering against my rib cage. "I'd like that too."

Aero looks like I've just given him the keys to a beachfront mansion in Malibu.

He plants a kiss on my lips and squeezes me extra hard.

I'm about to say more about the many things my insecurities would like me to air when the front door clangs open and Fern and Charlie come in, sopping wet but smiling. They get to our table and put their bags underneath before shaking off the rain and sliding into the booth. Our little section at the White Horse is turning into basecamp. I'm half expecting someone to pitch a tent.

"You two are looking rather cozy," Fern says with a grin that immediately makes me blush.

"The Yorkshire puddings here are great," I say sheepishly.

"Nice try changing the subject," Charlie says with a laugh. "You both look very happy together. I'd like to volunteer as flower girl for the big day."

Fern lets out a honking laugh, which sets me off, followed by Aero, then Charlie.

Before long we've finally caught our breath, and our waiter arrives, a stout man with a bristly mustache and stubby fingers.

"What can I get ya?" he says, his voice a deep bass.

We order a jug of elderberry juice, and the others get the same as me. The Yorkshire puddings *are* amazing.

"So, we're all ready?" Fern asks, looking between all of us. "Charlie, I've brought along this for you, not that I think we'll need it."

Fern places a small sword with an onyx stone embellished in the pommel.

"Bloody hell," Charlie says, shaking his head.

"Aero, I've gotten you this," Fern says, handing him a chainmail vest.

"Fern, how did you get all this stuff?" Aero asks, feeling the weight of the chainmail in his hands.

"I know people," Fern says simply, looking to me.

"I'm set, thanks," I say.

I take out the pouch from Gran. The others peer inside, and I watch as each of their eyes grow wider.

"So, I take it you're going to be taking the scale, then?" Charlie says, his voice showing just the slightest tremor.

"I guess," I say, looking to Aero, who suddenly has a concerned look on his face.

I give his thigh a squeeze to let him know it's all good as the waiter brings them their food and places the jug of elderberry juice in the center of the table.

"The main thing I think we need to remember," Fern says, taking a bite of her Yorkshire pudding and rolling her eyes back in delight, "is we need to trust each other. We all know what jobs we have to do to get that scale. We just need to trust that each of us knows what they're doing. We'll be fine."

Aero looks down at his Yorkshire pudding and prods it with his knife and fork.

"Trust sounds good," I say, feeling light for the first time in a while. "That's something I need work in. Trusting that the ones you lov—uh, care about—have your back."

Aero looks over at me and smiles, but I can see his mind working underneath the surface.

"Agreed," Fern says.

"Agreed," Charlie follows.

"Agreed," Aero says, putting his hand on top of mine and gently rubbing my knuckles.

Thirty

FELIX WASN'T LYING WHEN HE raved about these Yorkshire puddings. They really are next level.

I take another gravy-soaked bite and push my plate away as Fern, Charlie, Felix, and I all gather our things and head out into the night.

We take Fern's car, as it's the only vehicle between all of us that doesn't make weird noises or shudder when you brake. The air has turned cold, and Felix and I jump into the back seat as Fern and Charlie settle themselves up front, cranking the heating to full. Fern's car smells of cinnamon scrolls, old air fresheners, and dampness, but for some reason, it's strangely soothing.

I bundle Felix into a side-hug as the warmth from the heater engulfs us, and tiredness creeps over me.

Charlie adjusts the vents to ensure everyone gets their fair share of warm air before buckling his seatbelt.

Fern rubs her hands together in front of the heater and blows on them. "OK, we've got about three hours and forty-five minutes until we hit Draton."

"How far from Draton to Girton Falls?" I ask.

"We'll have to walk it, but I'd say about half hour," Charlie says as he fiddles with the radio. Some static breaks the silence before a track by The California Honeydrops come crackling through the speakers.

Fern releases the handbrake and turns the car toward the hills as we rumble off into the evening.

The smell of the warm air from the heater is replaced by the stink of oil as the bonnet starts to hum and dark smoke wafts out in giant clouds.

"Shit, shit, shit," Fern says as she stomps on the brakes, and we come to a stop on the side of the road.

"I'm no mechanic, but I don't think cars are supposed to bellow out black smoke," I say. I get out of the backseat and help Felix out too, the thick smoke causing us to splutter and choke.

Fern gives the driver's side door a kick before squatting and putting her head in her hands.

"OK, OK…" Charlie says, taking deep breaths. "Who else has a car?"

He looks between Felix and me expectantly.

"Nope," I say, shaking my head.

I look to Felix, who is also shaking his head, yet there's a glimmer of something in his eyes that I can't quite figure out.

"I don't have a car…" Felix says, deep in thought. "Fern, do you think we could leave this here?"

"For sure," Fern says with a choke. "It's as good as scrap metal, to be honest."

"What are you thinking?" I ask Felix as Charlie grabs our bags from within the car and hands them to each of us.

"I have an idea," Felix says.

WHEN WE GET TO AGGIE's house, all the lights are out except a flickering that looks like a candle in the top right window.

Felix opens the front door and beckons us inside.

"Where's your gran?" I ask, looking around.

"I'm not sure," Felix says. "Probably at the shop. She hangs out there late some nights."

I look to Fern and Charlie to see if they look as off as I feel, when Felix opens the cupboard in the corner.

"I'm not sure about taking your gran's car," Charlie says. He glances around the entryway and rubs his hands together to keep warm.

"We're not," Felix says, his words muffled from inside the closet as the sounds of clanging and thumping from within reach us. "I was thinking we could use these."

Felix opens the closet door farther to reveal four almost identical broomsticks.

I can't help but laugh. He looks kind of adorable standing there with four brooms, his eyes wide and his face excited, like a kid on Christmas Eve.

"Holy shit," Charlie says. He shakes his head and rolls his eyes to the ceiling and back.

"What?" Felix asks, his face losing its excitement.

I place my hand gently on the small of his back. "Felix, have you ever actually ridden a broom before?"

His eyes dart between all three of us, and a blush forms across the bridge of his nose. That blush!

"OK, well, no, but I... Do we have any other options?" Felix says, clearly flustered the longer we stand around staring at him.

Fern takes one of the broomsticks in her hand and surveys it, turning it over. "Solid oak. Birch twigs. These look pretty legit."

Charlie takes one and mounts it, looking between all of us with an expression full of more fear than when he was nearly drowned by a mermaid.

"Charlie, you can ride with me," Fern says.

"Wait, so we're actually going to take these?" I say, unclenching my jaw.

"Felix is right, we don't have any other options," Fern says as Charlie assesses the situation.

"Why do I need to ride with you?" Charlie asks, clearly ruffled.

I feel bad for Charlie, I really do, but he's not exactly a natural when it comes to magic, and I am completely on board with Fern's idea of them riding together.

"It's just easier," Fern says, looking to me for backup.

"Absolutely. Felix and I will ride together as well. It's safer and more practical."

Felix looks to me, and I think he gets what's going on, but to be sure, I throw him a wink and a smile.

Felix hands me a broom and double-checks that all our bags are secured. "OK, let's get going."

We all step out onto the porch and stare up into the black expanse of sky. The stars are out in the thousands, making the night look like a dazzling pool of diamonds.

Fern and I both hold our hands out next to our broomsticks, and they slowly shuffle and kick themselves to life. Fern's hovers up to waist height first and the two of them mount the broom slowly, Fern adjusting her weight to make sure the balance is correct.

My broom takes a few more shudders before it's hovering next to me and Felix, but I take a sigh of relief when I finally mount it and feel the sturdy heft of magic running through it.

"Hop on," I say to Felix, giving him my hand to hold as he throws a leg over and gets himself comfy.

Charlie is gripping Fern's shoulder and the broom with an iron claw, and it looks like he's using all his willpower to not faint.

"How will we know where we're going?" Felix asks as Fern and I both kick off. We all hover a few feet off the ground, swaying gently as we get used to the floating sensation.

Charlie opens his eyes. He smiles. "OK, this is *epic!*"

"I'll charm the broom to navigate us, and you can follow," Fern says, waving her hand softly over the oak handle as a pastel-green glow emanates throughout the birch twigs.

Felix's arms squeeze around me, and I swear I feel like I'm flying. Wait. We *are flying!*

Fern lets out a cheer as she and Charlie swoosh up and into the night.

I quickly turn around to give Felix a kiss before sending us high into the atmosphere, and we begin flying through the stars.

Thirty-One

THERE IS NO WAY TO describe the sensation of flying through a cloud on the back of a broomstick with your boyfriend.

Fern and Charlie zoom past and egg us on for a race. As Aero kicks the birch twigs, we shoot forward and up higher, the wind whipping our eyelashes and the smell of distant rain from the moisture in the air.

"Doing OK?" Aero asks, turning back to look at me briefly before steering us on.

I hug him tighter. The feelings I have for him are almost as difficult to explain as what it's like to fly. I'm nervous and giddy all at once. I know that I need to let go and trust it'll all be OK, but a constant nagging in the back of my mind is preventing me from completely falling for him.

I lean forward and peck him on the cheek. "More than OK."

We soar through the sky, across the tops of pine trees and over fields full of rows and rows of corn and sugarcane.

Fern spins her broomstick and hovers for a moment, waiting for us to catch up.

When Aero arrives next to her, he maneuvers our broom to do a skid like a car burnout before softly stalling midair as we bob softly in the night sky.

"Right," Fern says, wiping a dark lock of hair from her eyes and tucking it behind her ear. "Just over there is Draton. I say we find ourselves a place to sleep and recharge before getting up at dawn and heading to Girton Falls. Sound good?"

Both Aero and I give a thumbs-up, and Charlie nods in agreement behind Fern.

We drift through the trees on the outskirts of town and land with a light thump on a cobblestoned footpath leading to the town center.

When we get there, a few people are milling about outside, but for the most part, everyone is inside and away from the chilly night air.

"Wanna check that out?" Aero says, pointing to a dilapidated old building with the words THE MANOR in block letters across the crumbling brick entryway.

"Are you *trying* to get us killed?" I ask jokingly, giving him a gentle shove.

A cheeky grin forms across his face. "Scared?"

"I, uh… Don't know about—" Charlie starts.

Fern rolls her eyes. "Do you think you could put your big-boy pants on for just five minutes, Charlie? It was bad enough I had to lug you on the broomstick with me, but I—"

"Um… sorry?" Charlie says, looking at all of us individually. "I thought you said to come with you. I was happy getting there on my own, but you made it pretty clear you wanted me to ride with you."

The four of us stand motionless for a moment, the awkward-ness seeping through our little huddle like a bad smell.

"It's been a long few days," Aero says. "I think we all need a good cup of tea and some sleep. We'll be ready to go in the morning."

I smile, attempting to amp up the others, but they just shrug. Fern's eye-rolling continues as we all turn and head toward the Manor.

When we get inside, the warmth from the open fireplace in the corner of the room is the nicest greeting I could hope for. Considering the outside looks like a medieval slum, the inside is cozy and charming. The entryway is filled with plump armchairs and rugs with intricate patterns woven throughout. Next to the fireplace are rustic tables and chairs with men and women nursing steel mugs full of sweet mulled wine or spicy Irish coffee.

"Leave your bags here and go grab us a table. I'll be right back," Aero says.

Fern, Charlie, and I wander through to the main dining section and find a spot in the back near the fireplace.

Fern rubs her hands together as Charlie scoots in next to her at the table.

I run a fingernail along the wooden engravings across the tabletop and look at all the initials and hearts that have been carved over the years.

"I need food," Charlie says, prompting another eye roll from Fern.

Not wanting to stir the pot, I look back toward the entryway as Aero reappears and sits next to me, putting his hand on my thigh.

"All OK?" I ask, rubbing his knuckles.

"Yep. I've booked us a room and got us some hot tea and scones on the way."

Charlie smiles for the first time in a while, and relief washes across Fern's forehead.

"Thanks," Fern says, looking to Aero and then me. "I'm sorry for being in a mood."

Charlie looks to her and then back down at the table, clearly uncomfortable.

"It's fine, Fern. We know that it's been a big week. The main thing—" Aero starts as Fern shakes her head.

"No, it's not just that. It's just everything," Fern says, looking around the room, deep in her own thoughts. "It's a lot to process. People going missing, trying to study magic, wondering why Aggie was there that time, how to get a dragon scale without—"

"Wait, what did you just say?" I croak.

My stomach drops, and Aero looks like Fern has just smacked him across the face. Charlie seems to have frozen solid.

Nobody says anything, Fern just cups her hand over her mouth as her eyes widen.

"Fern. What did you just say?" I say again, this time slightly louder. I look across at Aero, who has yet to look, and then I turn back to face Fern. "Did you say my gran? What are you… *What* is going on?" I squeeze my nails into the palms of my hands.

"Felix, it's… We don't know exactly what—" Charlie starts, but I can't help but cut in.

"Wait, *we*?" I exclaim, my blood simmering under the surface of my skin. "What do you mean, we? Are you saying all of you know something? Or is it just Fern? Somebody better start talking."

The three of them start falling over each other's words, and I become more and more overwhelmed.

Aero slaps the table firmly with his hand. "Enough."

I take a deep breath, the waves of nausea coming and going like Dorset Harbor after a fishing boat has docked.

"Felix, I didn't know how to tell you," Aero says, knocking the remaining wind out of me and making the room spin.

I try to stand but wobble and end up sitting back down with a thump.

"T-Tell me what?" I ask, looking over at him and trying to not throw up.

Fern shakes her head, and Charlie looks like he wants to throw himself out the window behind him.

"The night of our date," Aero starts, pausing and taking a slow breath. "The girl we saw at the headland... The one who was taken—"

"I know, Aero," I say. "I saw her get taken by that thing. I remember—"

"I saw Aggie," Aero says, softer than I thought possible. "Standing over her in the woods."

His statement seems to physically hit me. My chest feels tight, and my whole body hums with anxiety.

"No," I say, doing my best to figure out what the hell is happening. "No, that's not possible. Besides, you would've already told me! We spoke about trust and... And you said that..."

It's too much. The room spins, and I clutch the edge of the table as I stand. "I have to go," I say, and I turn toward the door.

"Felix, wait. Please. We just need to complete the Revealion Spell, and we'll be able to know for sure," Fern says, standing to follow me.

"STOP!" I shout, drawing attention from the other patrons sitting nearby. "Do *not* follow me."

I turn and head for the door, slamming it shut behind me.

Thirty-Two

THAT LITERALLY COULD NOT HAVE gone worse. Not only are we in a random town in the middle of nowhere, trying to get a hold of a dragon scale, but now Felix has disappeared into the night.

I turn back and sit at our table as a pot of tea and some scones are placed in front of us.

Fern and Charlie are silent, and I don't even know where to begin. I feel physically sick.

To be honest, Felix is right. I should've told him sooner. It's weird that the one thing I was hoping to avoid has happened because I tried so hard to stop it from happening. Surely there's a metaphor in there somewhere. Something about going with the river instead of swimming against it? I dunno. What I *do* know is that Felix is pissed. Specifically, he's pissed at me, and I have no idea how to fix it.

Fern leans back in her seat. "Shit."

"Shit is right," Charlie says, taking a sip of his tea.

"I'm sorry for—" Fern starts.

"It's my fault," I say, more to myself than anyone else. "I just didn't want to make an already difficult situation more difficult."

I take another sip of tea and close my eyes, thinking of what to do next. I hate that this is happening. Felix deserves to know how important he is. How I'd never hurt him.

"Look, Felix will come around," Fern says, snapping back into action. "The main thing is getting that dragon scale. If you're right about Aggie having something to do with all of this, then he is in more danger than we know. You heard what Demelza said about a blood relative. We need to move fast!"

Fern's right. Regardless of how he feels about me, I won't let Felix get hurt.

"I need sleep," Charlie says, drowsily looking up to me.

I hand him and Fern their keys, and then I head out to look for Felix.

The town is much quieter than Dorset Harbor, and there aren't nearly as many streetlights. I pass the old fire department, the bakery, and a small store that seems to sell only tea cozies and watering cans.

At the florist on the corner, I turn left and find the outline of Felix sitting on a bench next to a small pond. I hesitate, my mind scrambling to think of something, anything, that will make sense. I need him to know I meant no harm.

"Can I sit?" I ask quietly, standing back enough to leave him alone, if that's what he really wants. "If you'd rather not speak at the moment, I understand." I take the key for the room out of my pocket and place it next to him before standing again. "I can leave you the key and leave you alone... I just really didn't want you to—"

"Aero, there was literally *one* thing I asked from you," Felix says, not turning to look at me. His voice is cold and tired, like it's a struggle to bother speaking at all.

"Felix, I swear—" I start.

"The thing is, I didn't need you to swear. I didn't need you to promise." His voice still soft and barely loud enough to hear. "I just wanted to trust you. I'm so clueless."

I take a step toward him, but he stands, still not looking at me, and takes a step toward the pond.

"I was simply hoping to find someone who respected me enough to not keep a secret," Felix says, kicking a pebble into the middle of the pond before turning and walking away.

I inhale slowly and try to keep it together. This is really bad.

I'm not going to cry. I'm not giving up. I know I've screwed up, but I did it from a place of love. That has to count for something.

When we finally perform the Revealion Spell, I know he's going to understand why I kept it from him. He'll see that I was trying to protect him.

In the meantime, I'm going to fix this and fix it soon. We have a dragon to find.

Thirty-Three

THIS IS WHAT I GET for trusting people. I am so pissed I could scream.

When I'm certain Aero is out of sight, I slump against a decaying archway made of brick and stone and put my head in my hands, trying to slow my breathing. The tears come hard and fast, and I smack the ground with balled-up fists.

Screw this. Why do I always let my guard down only to be proven right, that I shouldn't trust people? This is so typical.

I put a hand to my chest and count my breaths in and out to calm myself. Mum is my go-to person when I feel on the verge of a panic attack, but I know she has more than enough to worry and think about now without having me sobbing on the phone to her.

I scrunch up my forehead and stare up into the stars.

After I've finally calmed myself, I stand and dust the grass off my pants, and make my way back to the Manor. The downstairs area is empty, except for a few stray patrons nursing the last of their pints of Guinness.

I climb up the creaky stairwell to the hallway upstairs, where all the rooms branch off. My door opens to a small, cozy room with a single bed, a set of drawers, and a small desk with a writing pad and pen. Someone has brought my bags up and dumped them at the foot of my bed, and I sift through them to make sure my teaspoon is still safe and secure before crawling into bed and pulling the covers over me and drifting off to sleep.

When I wake, it's barely 6 AM. A cool draft of air wafts underneath the door and across the dusty floorboards.

I yawn and stretch before collecting my things and making my way downstairs, finding a seat next to the fireplace.

It's a DIY-type situation, so I pour myself a mug of black coffee from the giant pot sitting atop a trestle table and grab a few slices of toast with butter and strawberry jam before making my way back to my table.

Thankfully, the others are still asleep. I really don't feel like talking to any of them at the moment. Whatever they saw in the woods was either an illusion, or they got the wrong end of the stick. I know with every fiber of my being that Gran has absolutely nothing to do with what's going on in Dorset Harbor.

I spread the thick butter and bloodred strawberry jam across my sourdough toast and take a sweet, crunchy bite.

A few others who have stayed at the Manor make their way into the restaurant area, taking their cornflakes, yogurt, and coffee to tables and opening dog-eared books or newspapers, barely taking any notice of me.

I open my backpack and fumble around for *Incantations, Herbs & Astrology* but realize after some serious digging that it's not there. I think back to the last time I was reading it and focus my mind to where I think it could be before plunging my hand back into my backpack and searching for it in my mind's eye. I feel the worn leather hardcover across my fingertips and grab hold of it, pull it up and out through some dimension in the bottom of my bag, and place it on the table in front of me.

I open to the chapter on taming a dragon and take a deep breath. Most of the information I find is around Charlie's method of putting the dragon to sleep with bewitched fireflies. My hands clam up as I read the end of the paragraph: *Just four people in recorded history have been successful at bewitching a dragon with fireflies for long enough to escape with their lives.*

I take a deep breath in and give myself a shake to clear my mind as Aero peeks his head around the corner, followed by Fern and Charlie. Aero looks translucent, and both Fern and Charlie keep their heads focused on the scratchy carpet throughout the room.

I avoid eye contact with any of them as they grab a coffee each and make their way to the table directly in front of me. I keep my head directed at *Incantations, Herbs & Astrology* and pretend to read the passage I've already read four times. I take a sip of my coffee and go to take a bite of my toast when I realize the strawberry jam has separated itself from the butter to form a simple *Hello* across the surface.

I conceal a smile. I know what Aero's doing, and I'm not buying it.

I take a sharp bite through the H and look back down at the paragraph to give it a read for the fifth time.

At first, I think a migraine is looming, but then the letters on the page rearrange themselves in front of me.

You look kinda cute when you're mad...

I slam the book shut and stuff it in my backpack, preparing to stand.

"Felix, wait," Aero says, making his way over and taking the seat next to me.

"I don't want to talk to you," I say, avoiding eye contact as best as I can. The last thing I need is to gaze into those ridiculously beautiful multicolored irises of his.

"Listen, I know what I did wasn't the smartest thing..."

I scoff, shaking my head.

"But," Aero continues, placing his hand on top of mine. "I didn't know how to talk to you about it, and I was so scared of hurting you. I was worried you'd react like this."

I look behind him briefly to Fern and Charlie, who have timid expressions on their faces.

"Do you think my gran has something to do with... with all this?" I ask, looking into his eyes for the first time and not daring to blink.

"I," Aero starts, refusing to break eye contact with me either. "No. I mean, I don't think..."

I shake my head, anger boiling in my gut.

"Felix, please. How can *any* of us be sure about *anything* right now?" Aero pleads.

I hate that he's right, but I'm not willing to tell him that. Whatever is happening, I need it to be over. This can't keep going on.

We need to find the dragon.

Thirty-Four

It's been three hours since we left Draton and I still don't think we're any closer to finding Girton Falls.

Fern suggested we leave our broomsticks back at the Manor and head to the falls by foot, but I insisted. Considering they're already wary of my moods, they relented to meeting in the middle and carrying them in case we need them.

"I'm starving," Charlie says, squinting at the afternoon sun as we make our way through an overgrown canopy of bush and into a small forest.

"Here," Aero says, handing Charlie a scone.

"Thanks," Charlie says, closing his eyes and snapping his fingers.

After a few snaps, I can't help myself.

"You OK, Charlie?" I ask, looking to the others to make sure he hasn't completely lost his mind.

"I'm trying to…" He snaps again. "Add butter and—" Snap, snap. "Jam, but—"

Aero snaps his fingers behind his back so Charlie can't see, and moments later, the scone begins to shimmer with butter, followed by rosy red jam.

"There we go," Charlie says, pleased with himself yet none the wiser that Aero helped him out.

We head through another thicket, and Fern hums to herself, occasionally checking her map to make sure we're on the right track.

I've been keeping my distance from the others because I have no idea how I feel about any of them right now. Aero keeps looking over at me with a timid smile, but I can't bring myself to return it. I can't believe he wouldn't tell me something like that. None of it makes sense, and every time I think about it, my blood starts to boil.

"OK," Fern says, shielding her eyes from the sun and looking around the clearing we've found ourselves in. "I think we have another mile or two to go before we'll get to the base of the falls."

Charlie leans down and puts his hands on his knees, taking a break and breathing slowly as sweat pours from his forehead.

Aero takes a gulp of water from a bottle in his bag and offers it to me, which I decline out of pettiness; I'm extremely thirsty, but he doesn't need to know that. Instead, I focus on a bottle of water from the fridge back home and lift it from the vortex I create in my backpack.

Aero doesn't notice the weird quantum leap magic I'm performing and instead continues on the path toward the falls.

When we finally get to the base of Girton Falls, we are all exhausted.

The falls are enormous, sending a cascade of glittering water down a huge cliff face. A small cave is carved behind it, about fifty feet above us.

Charlie is the color of the red pebbles that litter the ground around us. Fern is clutching the stitch in her side, and Aero collapses in a heap, using his backpack as a pillow. I, on the other hand, am running on adrenaline and resentment, two things that are definitely not the best combo for someone looking for a dragon.

I look at the giant cliff face to figure out how I'll get to the cave behind the falls without immediately disturbing the dragon.

"Can I have the broom?" I ask Aero.

"What?" Aero says, opening his eyes and looking over at me with his hand outstretched, shielding his face from the sun.

"I said, can I have the broom? I'd like to go and get this over and done with." I can barely make eye contact with him.

"Felix, you can't be serious," Fern says, standing guard over her broom as if I'm about to snatch it off her.

"I'm about as serious as they come," I say, looking to Aero and waiting for him to hand over the broom.

Aero sits up. "We came here together. We're going to get the dragon scale *together*."

A tremble runs through me. "That was *before* I realized you'd all been lying to me."

"Felix, we didn't lie to you," Charlie says.

I look to Aero, and I know I'm being an asshole, but at the same time, I feel it's warranted. I needed him to prove to me that I could trust him. This is the exact opposite of what I hoped for.

"Fine," I say, rolling my eyes. I sit down and glance between all three of them as I try to steady my breath.

I look back up to the falls. Where is the dragon now? From down here, you'd never know an enormous scaly monster was lurking behind the curtain of water.

Charlie unpacks his backpack as Fern begins to pitch a tent for all of us, and by 'pitch' I mean clap her hands counterclockwise and speak a simple incantation under her breath. The tent pops to life, as if someone is punching it into place from the inside out. The canopy takes shape as the tent poles connect themselves into place, the invisible force securing everything nicely into the crumbling red dirt around us.

"Perfect," Fern says with a simple nod before opening the hatch and going inside.

I take my belongings and follow behind her, only to find that the inside is the furthest thing from any tent I've ever seen.

"You've got to be kidding," I say, looking around.

I step into a long hallway that leads to a perfectly quaint little kitchen. A fridge, oven, and small wooden table with a red and white tablecloth sit neatly in the center. Off the hallway are doorways (yes, doorways) to various other bedrooms, living rooms, and bathrooms. It looks like a five-star hotel.

I shake my head as Aero and Charlie each make their way inside, find a bedroom that suits them, and throw their belongings inside.

Aero gives me a look as he heads into his room that I think may be an invitation to join him while we stay here, but I don't think I'm in the best headspace to act like nothing is bothering me right now.

I open the bedroom door closest to the front entrance and throw my stuff inside, clocking the broomstick Aero left standing next to the front door.

The others are all in various stages of unpacking and I'm all out of fucks to give.

I grab the broomstick and head outside, ready to take on a dragon.

Thirty-Five

IT TAKES A BEAT LONGER than normal for me to realize I'm staring at the space in the hallway where I left the broomstick.

Fern puts a hand lightly on my arm.

"You OK?" she asks.

I go to speak when I see Fern's eyes grow wide as she makes a dash to the entryway of the tent.

Barely thinking, I follow her outside and wait for my eyes to adjust to the darkening afternoon light.

"FELIX!" Fern shouts as Charlie joins us outside.

I look up to see Felix hovering and bucking like a rodeo cowboy atop the broomstick, slowly making his way toward the cave in the falls.

"*Shit!*" I scream before running back into the tent.

I'm closely followed by Fern and Charlie, who both look like they could faint and scream simultaneously.

Charlie dashes into his room, arriving moments later with his jar of fireflies.

I finally find Fern's broom tucked away next to the fridge and run back outside, the others right on my tail.

"Here," Charlie says, handing me the jar of fireflies.

Fern paces back and forth, looking up to make sure Felix hasn't crashed into the mountain or bucked into the forest below.

"Felix, wait there! I'm coming!" I shout.

I kick off and let the broom cut through the air like a blade, sending me high into the treetops yet far away enough from Felix to not cause more trouble.

Felix bobs once or twice nearby, but I'm too far away to reach him. I'm at a decent distance to catch him if he falls, but the longer he's in the air, the more control he has over the broom. He edges toward the cave within the falls, and my heart jolts up into my throat as I remember there's a dragon in there.

"FELIX!" I scream again.

I edge my broom toward him as he enters the cave through the falls and into the blackness beyond.

I follow him through the wall of water and land with a thump, shaking my drenched hair out of my eyes and giving myself a pat down to dry off.

As my eyes finally adjust, I see Felix crouched in a corner, his broom by his side and his body rigid. His arms are out to his sides, like he's balancing on an invisible tightrope.

"Felix?" I say into the darkness, only to be met by a piercing *SHH.*

When my eyes adjust, I see why. In front of Felix sits a dragon the size of a Mini Cooper, its dark-green scales glisten with a translucent shade of purple, and its head reveals two nostrils that puff smooth clouds of dark smoke like an old steam train.

It's only when I look farther into the cave that I realize this car-sized dragon is in fact just the infant.

Lying on a mossy granite ledge a little farther inside sits an enormous beast about the size of a navy ship. Its huge leathery wings are tucked into its sides, and the tail seems to curve into the deepest reaches of the cave.

I take a slow inhale, desperate not to move or make a sound.

Felix turns to look at me and mouths the words *I've got this.*

I shake my head and lift my palms to him, gesturing for him to stop, but he's already treading lightly toward the infant dragon, each step making the slightest scratch on the gravel floor.

Barely thinking, I grab the jar of fireflies and lift them to show Felix in the darkness, my hand hovering over the lid, ready to unleash them.

He waves me off and takes another step, his concentration completely on the tail in front of him.

I hold my breath as he makes his way closer, the only sounds coming from his treads and the roaring water of the falls.

He finally gets to a section of cave where he can crouch close enough to the dragon without having to keep walking.

He gives me a thumbs-up and takes a breath, steadying himself on the rocks surrounding him.

I return the thumbs-up as he leans forward and reaches down toward the tail of the dragon.

I hear my heartbeat kicking against my rib cage, and I place my hand over my chest to calm myself.

I feel like I've been watching for hours when Felix finally sits back, throwing his hand into the air and brandishing the shimmering purple scale.

I give him two thumbs-up in the air before beckoning

him toward me, constantly looking back at the infant and the enormous beast behind.

Felix tucks the shimmering scale into his pocket and moves slowly across the uneven ground.

Grabbing my broom, I edge toward the exit of the cave, and then I hear it.

The piercing sound of foot on crumbling rock.

I turn quickly to see Felix's eyes wider than I thought possible, his left ankle deep in a mound of crushed stone while his right hangs midair, unsure where to step next.

Before I can think, the infant dragon's tail moves like that of a lizard adjusting in the sun.

I hold my breath as Felix turns to face the dragon head-on.

It blinks once, its fiery red eyes summing Felix up as its large nostrils inhale sharply three times in a row.

As the reptilian head bows forward to get a closer look, I hear the first terrifying sounds of movement from the beast behind.

"RUN!" Felix screams, his broom out of reach as he leaps across a boulder and heads toward me, arms outstretched as I mount the broom.

I'm about ready to kick off into the air when I feel a lick of heat behind me; a billowing wall of fire is being unleashed in our direction.

"QUICK!" I shout as Felix reaches me, turning to watch as his broom is engulfed in flames and turned to cinders.

I kick off and we ascend, my only thought being *Get the hell out of this cave.* I turn right to avoid a boulder that is crashing in front of us and veer toward the left of the exit.

"Wait!" Felix screams, tapping me hard on the shoulders. "Wait, I need to go back!"

"You can't!" I scream, edging closer to the exit.

"I left my teaspoon back there!"

"We'll get you another one! We *have* to get out of here!"

"NO!" Felix says, shifting his balance and nearly sending both of us into the cave wall as he jumps off and lands with a thud, right next to the infant dragon and directly in front of its mother.

Thirty-Six

LANDING WITH A THUMP, I run across the uneven terrain as fast as my legs will carry me and scoop up my backpack, checking to make sure my teaspoon is inside. The remains of my toasted broomstick lay nearby, and while I try to think of a way to get out of this cave, I feel a warm breath of air next to me.

I turn to face the infant dragon, its giant eyes taking me in. It's weirdly beautiful, the scales shimmering like they've been dipped in liquid silver. Strangely, I'm not scared at all. It's as if I've met her before. She seems familiar, like an old family member or a pet from childhood.

"Hey," I say, taking a step forward and slowly reaching my hand out, trying not to disturb her.

She dips her head and allows me to place my palm on her. It's rough and solid, like a giant iron ball, and I slowly caress the scales, showing I mean no harm.

I flick through my memory, trying to remember if I've ever come across something like her before when it hits me. I remember the dragon I saw printed in a page in *Incantations, Herbs & Astrology*. It was a beautiful young dragon named Papaver that lived hundreds of years ago and was believed to have guarded the Tower of London. She had the same purple scales, the same beautiful eyes as this one in front of me.

"Papaver," I say, almost to myself.

I don't know how much time has passed when I finally hear Aero: "FELIX! GET OUT OF THERE!"

Aero is just outside the cave's entrance, past the falls and hovering on his broom.

I turn to see Papaver's mother crashing through the cave's pillars and heading right for me.

Thinking fast, I turn and make a run for the cave's exit, looking back once to see Papaver squaring off with its parent. It stops me in my tracks as my new friend lets out a bone-chilling roar, sending a trail of fire in the direction of the enormous beast before her.

Turning back toward the falls, and my way out, I pick up the pace, heading straight for Aero, who has his hand outstretched and his broom steady and waiting for me. I'm about to make a jump for it when I'm bucked into the air like I've been hit by a semitrailer.

I land with a crack and find myself gripping to the hard, scaly surface of Papaver as she whisks us through the cascading falls and out into the crisp air, leveling out smoothly next to Aero.

"Holy shit!" Aero says, his mouth failing to stay shut as he looks at me and the dragon I'm suddenly riding.

"I have no idea what's going on," I say, catching my breath as I find the grooves in Papaver's scales and hook my fingers to grip.

"Felix! She's..." Aero says, his face beaming and his voice faltering.

"She's what?" I ask, placing a hand on my chest to slow my breathing.

"Your familiar," Aero says, unable to wipe the smile off his face as he leads us back to the base of the falls and lands softly. Papaver drifts to a small patch nearby and lands smoothly before curling her wings into her sides.

I hop off and give her a stroke.

"Are you really my fa—" I stop myself, looking into her eyes. "Family. We're family." I say quietly, just for her to hear. "Thank you for saving me."

Papaver rests her head gently on my shoulder, almost like a hug, before curling herself neatly and closing her eyes for a much-needed nap.

When I get to the tent, Aero, Fern, and Charlie are all sitting outside around a fire Charlie is attempting to ignite.

"Hi," I say. The resentments I'd hidden in the back corner of my mind come back to remind me I'm still not happy with any of them.

They each wave, smiling sheepishly.

"Aero told us you got the scale," Fern says, poking a stick into the firepit and sending a flame through the base, so Charlie thinks it was him.

I shrug.

"It would've been much less hassle if we'd known your familiar was going to be a dragon!" Charlie says with a grin, clearly trying to break the ice.

"Your fireflies will come in handy next time," Aero says, patting Charlie on the arm as he finds himself a seat by the crackling fire.

I turn toward the tent. "Well, I think I'll hit the hay."

"Felix, wait," Aero says, standing momentarily, as if considering whether to approach me.

I face him and let my shoulders fall. It's too difficult being this pent up and angry. I can feel the anger dissipating and being replaced with a cold disappointment in the base of my gut.

"Please, don't be mad at me," Aero says, his voice softer than usual and his body slumped and defeated.

"I'm not mad," I say, looking anywhere but at him for fear I'll burst into tears. "I just thought I was worth... more than that. I..." I breathe before facing him properly, taking a moment to really look into his eyes. "We'll have our answers soon. Let's get home first thing tomorrow and start this Revealion Spell. I need answers."

Aero nods while Fern and Charlie sit quietly behind him.

I turn and head inside, locking myself in my little bedroom and peering outside to check on Papaver briefly before I curl into a ball on my bed and drift off to sleep.

THE FIRST THING I HEAR upon waking is the sound of pots and pans being battered to pieces.

I go down the hallway and into the kitchen to find Charlie and Fern making one hell of a spread. Charlie is stacking the table with deviled eggs, sausages, hash browns, and baked beans. Fern is in the middle of making a stack of pancakes and crispy rashers of bacon.

"Morning," I say, taking a seat at the table. "Where's Aero?" I decide not to sound too enthused. I don't want him getting the wrong idea.

"Gone for a walk. He said he needed to clear his head," Charlie says, taking a bite of a dry slice of toast.

I load up my plate with everything I can and pour a glass of cold orange juice before the others join me at the table.

Fern stirs her coffee and focuses on the whirlpool her spoon makes. "We haven't had a chance to properly talk."

"There's not a lot to really talk about," I say. I take a bite of a sausage and wash it down with some juice.

Charlie glances over at Fern before rapping his fingers on the table.

"We know it wasn't the right thing to do," Charlie says, his voice trembling a bit. "But we're all pretty scared at the moment. There's no guidebook on how to deal with missing teenagers in your hometown. We don't know what to believe or what the hell is going on."

I let the words sink in and feel myself loosening up. I know how scary all of this has been. I've been going through it too. To be honest, if roles were reversed, I'd probably have done the exact same thing.

"Well, I'm sorry," I say, almost under my breath.

"We are too," Fern replies, leaning over and tapping my hand softly. "Go give that boyfriend of yours a hug. He's barely slept, and he cares about you so much. Go kiss and make up, or whatever it is you two would prefer to do in this soundproof magic tent I created."

I can't help but laugh. "You're filthy," I say, giggling to myself as I head outside to look for him.

"Aero!" I call, making my way around to the back of the tent and finding Papaver sitting upright and stretching her beautiful, long, scaly neck toward some apples in the tree above. I pat her flank a few times before making my way into the undergrowth, following the trail of footsteps Aero left behind.

The morning light is golden and casts the most beautiful patterns across the trees and shrubbery. Occasional rabbits and foxes dart across the path in search of food or shelter, and I take it all in, moment by moment, as I go deeper into the forest.

I get to a section of the path that leads in both directions and try to figure out which way looks more trodden.

"Felix!" I hear from behind me.

I turn to find Aero walking toward me, his face beaming when he realizes I've come looking for him.

"I'm sorry," I say, shaking my head.

"No way!" Aero says, smiling bigger with every step closer to me. "I'm sorry. I'm just so glad you're talking to me. I really can't tell you how much I—"

It's as if time has stopped, and things move in dreamlike slow-motion. A dark creature appears from above, blocking out the warm glow of the sun and descending on us like something from a nightmare.

A claw grips Aero around the waist, yanking him hard off his feet.

"NO!" I scream, running as fast as I can toward him.

I scream again, but nothing comes out. I go into shock as I see the creature lift Aero farther into the sky, up past the treetops, and away into the distance.

Thirty-Seven

IT TAKES ME A WHILE to realize Fern and Charlie are with me. My heart hammers harder in my chest with every breath I take.

"It's Aero," I splutter, my voice raspy and tired. "He—"

"We know," Charlie says, gripping my shoulder. "We saw it happen."

Fern shakes her head. "We have to go. Right now." She turns and splays her hands open wide in the direction of the tent, sending it in on itself and compacting together swiftly to the size of a backpack.

Within ten minutes, we are on our way home, sitting steadily atop Papaver and flying over the treetops. I steer her gently toward the cliffs on the outskirts of town near the lighthouse and give her a stroke along her neck, promising to come back shortly.

The three of us gather our things and run toward the library.

"I'll meet you guys there," Fern says, making a beeline for her place.

"Me too—I need to get the remaining ingredients from the shop," I say.

Charlie makes his way toward the library while I check my backpack again to make sure the mermaid hair and Papaver's scale are tucked away securely before taking the old cobblestoned road toward the Silver Teacup.

When I arrive, it's empty, the only light coming from a flickering candle on the shop counter, and neither Gran nor Winifred are anywhere to be found. I open the big wooden door with a creak and step into the dusty darkness.

"Hello?" I shout, my voice bouncing from wall to wall and echoing into the back room.

Nobody returns my call, so I go behind the counter and search for the missing ingredients.

I find what I'm looking for fairly quickly, my mind drifting to Aero whenever I let it. The thought of him being carried away, the sound of his scream, just won't leave my mind.

I grab the eye of newt, some mugwort, lavender, and poppy seeds and pour them all into a muslin bag, tying it gently with string and placing it into my backpack. I take another quick look around the empty shop before closing the big front door and heading toward the library.

The big stone building waits for me, a dark-purple storm cloud floating above, staring down at me menacingly. I walk up the entryway steps, through the reception area, and toward the back of the fiction section, where we had our meeting the other day. The library itself seems practically deserted, the few people I see burying their heads in dusty books with mottled paper.

When I get to the end of the fiction section, Charlie is pacing back and forth deep in thought.

"Hey, Charlie," I say, putting my backpack down and emptying the ingredients onto a table.

"Hey," he says. He counts his footsteps on the marble floor and fiddles with the string on his hoodie.

I open my bag again and focus my mind on the small copper cauldron that sits on our kitchen bench at home.

Charlie looks over as I pull the cauldron from within my bag and place it in front of him, the bronze being shiny enough to show his reflection back to him.

"Neat," Charlie says.

Fern arrives moments later, pushing her dark hair behind her ears and placing the old tome on the table next to the ingredients and cauldron.

"OK, let's get this over with," Fern says.

I put my hand on the cover of the tome, and sparks run through me.

Fern opens it up to the Revealion Spell and takes a slow breath in.

"Here, add this to the cauldron first," Fern says, handing me a small jug. "Lamb's milk."

I empty the jug into the cauldron and rearrange the remaining ingredients.

"Now start adding the ingredients in one at a time while chanting—"

"Wait," comes a voice from behind us, one I instantly recognize.

"Gran!" I shout, moving toward her and bringing her in for a hug. "Where have you been? I haven't spoken to you in forever."

Gran looks between me, Fern, and Charlie and smiles timidly.

Fern and Charlie have lost color in their face, and weirdly enough, I feel their anxiety attaching onto me.

"Gran? What is going on?" I say, taking a step back automatically.

"Felix, there is a lot more to all this than you can imagine," Gran says, shaking her head.

My stomach tightens, my mind doing everything it can to keep up.

"Felix, get away from her," another voice shouts from farther back in the fiction section. I recognize that voice, but it doesn't make sense until I see Blythe standing in front of me.

"Blythe, Aero's been taken. We wanted to—" I start, stopping immediately as Blythe gets closer, her hand raised and an expression on her face that I can't quite read.

"I know," Blythe says, looking at Gran while at the same time keeping her distance. "Aggie, where is my grandson?"

Gran looks to Blythe and back to me, and I go cold.

"Gran, please tell me you—"

"Felix, stay out of this," Blythe says, directing her gaze at Gran as she takes a step closer. "Aggie, your grandson knows all about what you've been up to. My grandson made sure of that. Now you need to tell me where he is."

"What?" I say, practically shouting.

"Oh, you didn't know?" Blythe says, her face contorting into a grimace. "Your gran kidnapped my grandson for her own wicked pleasure. You surely can add the rest up by now, dear boy."

"Gran, please tell me what's going on," I say, my voice quivering.

The disappearing teens, Aero claiming to have seen Gran in the woods—all of it makes me feel sick.

"Now," Blythe says, honing in on Gran. "*Where* is my grandson, Aggie Silver?"

Gran sizes Blythe up, clearly miffed that she used her last name in a sentence.

"You know I can't tell you that," Gran says, clutching both of her hands together in protest. "Blythe Carling."

"Gran, what are you saying?" I say, my whole body trembling. This can't be happening.

I saw *something* take Aero. It wasn't Gran, I know that for sure.

"Felix, darling, trust me when I say I would never ever hurt you," Gran says, not taking her eyes off Blythe.

My legs go weak as Fern and Charlie appear on either side of me.

"Felix, I think I understand what's going on," Fern whispers to me under her breath. "Remember what Demelza said about the final spell needing a blood relative in love? That must be you and Aero!"

My world slowly unravels, and the room start to spin. This is too much. I can't figure it out fast enough, and I feel like I could vomit.

"*Why* would my gran capture Aero, though?" I whisper through clenched teeth. "To steal his youth?"

I glance over at Gran, who is staring at me, her face pale and the slightest smile in the corner of her mouth.

"To protect him," Gran says, her voice calmer than I've ever heard it.

It takes me a moment for Gran's words to sink in.

"You silly old woman," Blythe says. She lifts her hand high into the air.

For a second, I think Blythe is going to smack Gran across the face, but instead, she swings her hand down, causing an enormous gust of wind and a crack of green light to throw Gran high into the air, across the library, and land her with a crash against the bookcase near the exit.

"Blythe Carling," Fern says quietly to herself.

"What?" Charlie asks, his voice quaking and his legs noticeably trembling.

"Not *Curling*. Carling! From the book! Mirabelle Silver! *It was the Carling woman, remember?*" Fern's face drops, and fear shimmers in her eyes.

It all makes sense and hits me like a ton of bricks as I glance up at Blythe to find her staring back with bloodred eyes and a wolfish, terrifying grin.

The next thing I see is a flash of blinding green light, and I feel my body tumbling through the air until darkness envelops me.

Thirty-Eight

I WAKE TO THE SMELL of burning.

When my eyes finally adjust, I see a stack of autobiographies smoldering next to a toppled bookcase that I must've crashed through. My back is stiff, and my head feels like I've done ten rounds with Muhammad Ali, but I'm grateful I can still walk.

I shove a few scattered copies of old nature books off me and sift through the rubble to find Fern and Charlie nearby. Their eyes are closed, but they're still breathing. I give both of them a nudge, but they are out cold.

Pulling myself up, I hear my back crack a few times as I limp over to the table where our ingredients sit untouched.

Grabbing some sprigs of mugwort, I remember a passage from *Incantations, Herbs & Astrology* and rub the plant between my palms.

When I get to Fern and Charlie, I sprinkle the mugwort across the bridges of their noses and softly speak the word "*Surgit*" over and over.

Eventually, Fern's right eye begins to flicker, followed by her left. Charlie isn't too far behind, and before long, the pair are sitting up, stretching out their bruised and battered bodies, and surveying the damage around us.

"Gran," I say. I pick myself up and force my body across the long expanse of hallway to where Gran lies in a heap next to a toppled bookcase.

I perform the mugwort again for Gran, and she eventually wakes, blinking rapidly while adjusting her disheveled hair as fast as she can.

"Darling," Gran says, pulling me in for a hug. "I'm so sorry I didn't tell you sooner."

Fern and Charlie crawl in next to us, and Fern manifests a large jug of cold water from thin air, handing it gently to Gran, who takes a long gulp before passing it around.

"How long have you known?" I ask, stroking her hand gently.

My mind is running a million miles an hour, but the soft touch of Gran's hand and her signature perfume immediately calms me down.

"Too long," Gran says, massaging a cramp in her leg. "Demelza and I... We had our suspicions. That day Blythe arrived in town with her ridiculous shoe shop."

"Is Delemza OK?" Charlie asks, taking a swig from the water jug.

"As far as I know, she's fine," Gran says. "It was her who told me I'd find you here. Those cards of hers are rather powerful."

I shake my head and steady my breathing.

"I just don't understand why Aero's own grandma... would... would try to..." I can't finish the sentence because it's too much to take in.

Gran looks at the cracked ceiling. "I know."

"But what about the girl in the woods?" Fern asks, biting the nail on her pinky.

"My dear," Gran says with a simple shrug. "I was trying to help, but I feel I may have just made things worse."

I lean across and hold Gran's hand, gently stroking her knuckles. "Not possible. You're amazing."

Gran's eyes mist over, and she wipes the tears away, sniffing once and shaking it off. "Blythe has been around for centuries." Gran looks at her hands and sighs. "All the way back to Mirabelle. Demelza and I have heard rumors for years but have never had the... pleasure of meeting her, until now."

"And Aero wasn't aware?" Charlie asks, his brow furrowing.

Gran shakes her head. "Not in the slightest. That's what makes Blythe so dangerous."

I look around at the wreckage of torn books and tattered papers and feel very small. I clutch Gran's hand tighter. "What do we do now?"

"Blythe is probably looking for Aero as we speak."

"We need to stop her," Charlie says, his voice the strongest I've heard it since our mermaid encounter.

Fern jumps up, dusts herself off, and runs to the opposite end of the room. After rummaging around the contents of her backpack, she pulls out her tome and hauls it over to us, opening it with a thud to a passage on *Conquering Darkness*.

"Wow, they don't beat around the bush with these books, do they?" Charlie says with a grin.

I glance over the chapter. My heart sinks. "I'm not powerful enough to perform any of this. Blythe has been doing this for centuries. How am I going to defeat her when I've only just learned how to pull things out of my bag?"

Fern, Charlie, and Gran look at me, and I can read the expressions on their faces. They don't know either.

"I'm doing this alone," I say, my heart hammering against my chest. "It's bad enough Aero's own grandmother is behind all of this. I'm not letting you lot get hurt too."

I slam the tome shut and stand, my whole body thrumming with adrenaline.

I open my backpack and grab the one thing I know I need: my teaspoon.

"Gran, I'm sorry," I say, tears prickling underneath the surface of my eyelids.

"Darling, whatever for?" Gran says, her beautiful smile instantly calming me.

"For doubting you for even a second," I say, letting a rogue tear escape and roll down my cheek.

Gran pats my hand tenderly before shaking herself and smiling through glistening eyes. "I am *so* proud of you, my special boy. Now, go get that boyfriend of yours. I've taken him to the lighthouse. He'll be safe there."

Fern and Charlie look like they're about to say something, but I instead watch a confused expression crawl across their faces.

"What?" I ask, following their line of sight.

"Thanks, Aggie," a cold, translucent voice says from behind me.

When I turn, I finally see what Fern, Charlie, and my gran are staring at in horror.

Blythe's bloodred lips are hovering right behind me, the rest of her clearly invisible.

"Shit," I say, clutching my teaspoon in my pocket.

By the time I've turned around properly to confront her, she has evaporated into thin air.

"I have to go," I say. I lean into hug everyone individually before making a run for the door and out into the unknown.

Thirty-Nine

THE WIND IS HOWLING WHEN I finally make it to the cliff, great gusts tearing branches from trees and lifting patches of grass from the uneven terrain. I stare up the lighthouse, it's giant beam casting a golden glow over the treacherous sea below, and I try to gather myself.

I battle against the wind and eventually make it to the entrance, heaving in my breaths as my lungs fight the gale force winds. The door to the lighthouse is locked, so I race around back to where the keeper's cottage sits and rattle the rusty door handle. When no reply comes, my stomach drops.

The cottage has a small yellow light that flickers occasionally, so I follow it and head to the back window, watching my footing in case Blythe is nearby.

I find a rusty old barrel leaning up against the cottage and pull it underneath the window before retrieving my teaspoon and pointing it at the glass.

"*Convello*," I say as a thin gold light erupts from the end of my teaspoon, knocking out the glass with a smash.

"AERO?" I shout, lifting myself up onto the barrel and crawling through the window space, dropping with a clonk onto the stone floor below.

"F-Felix?" Aero calls, tentatively and quietly.

I look around as my eyes adjust to the pale light and realize it's more like a barn than an actual cottage. I've landed in a small bedroom with a simple queen-sized bed and a shag rug.

As I walk into the only other room, I realize the light is coming from a single bulb hanging on a cord in the corner, swaying in the drafty wind creeping underneath the ceiling.

Aero is getting up from the dusty couch next to an unlit fireplace as I enter the room, his face sunken and frightened.

"Felix, I... I don't know what to—"

"Come here," I say, bringing him into a hug and squeezing him tight.

"I'm so sorry I ever suggested Aggie. This really hurts," Aero says, visibly trembling but doing his best to hold it together.

His breathing slowly calms as I stroke his back. My mind runs through a thousand different scenarios as I try to figure out what to do next.

"I can't believe we didn't even need to perform the Revealion Spell... We found out regardless," Aero says, shaking his head and choking out a laugh.

"The main thing is we know what's going on now. We just need to figure out what to do about it," I say.

I check that all the doors are bolted shut.

I flick my teaspoon in the direction of the fireplace and send a spark, which turns into a blazing fire moments later, filling the room with a soft golden light and some much-needed heat.

"Do you want something to eat?" I ask. I sit down next to Aero again and hold out my hand, which he takes.

"I'm starving, but this place is empty," Aero says, looking around at the bareness of it all.

"It's a good thing I'm getting better at magic," I say with a wink. I stand and walk over to the pantry cupboard, which I open and place my arm in, focusing on what I think is needed at a time like this.

Aero cranes his neck, as if he's trying to get a better view. "Have you found Narnia in there or something? I didn't realize it was such a deep cupboard."

"It's not," I say, pulling out a teapot full of chai and a plate of warm chocolate chip cookies.

I sit next to Aero and hand him the plate of cookies.

"You're getting good, babe," Aero says, giving me a kiss.

I pour us each a cup of chai. "It's pretty infantile magic overall. Basic party magic, nothing too exciting or dangerous, I guess."

"Well, I'm more than happy to avoid dangerous at the moment," Aero replies. "We've been tiptoeing around that for quite some time."

Aero takes a bite of his gooey chocolate chip cookie.

I open my mouth to say something but stop myself. I don't want to ruin this right now. We've had enough drama and surprises for one week, and I think if I try to dissect the many nightmarish reasons why Blythe is hell-bent on sucking the youth from teens in Dorset Harbor, it'll send me crazy.

So I wrap my arm around Aero and bring him closer, letting his curly hair cushion the side of my head and both the smell of cinnamon from the chai and the lavender from Aero himself soothe me.

Aero takes a slow sip of his tea. "So, what's the plan now?"

I giggle. Clearly my plans at avoiding that conversation were never going to last long.

"I'm not entirely sure," I say, looking around the dilapidated old cottage. "We could move in here permanently?" I ask jokingly. "You know, live off the land. Start a vegetable garden out back. You could start writing books while I stand next to the lighthouse for days on end, looking out at the horizon while Enya plays in the background."

Aero pinches the bridge of his nose and shakes his head. "You're ridiculous."

"The best people in life usually are," I say, and take a sip of chai. "So? What do you honestly think of my plan? Too much?"

"No, I think I'd love that. We would just need a car to venture into town, in camouflage obviously, to buy essentials every now and then."

I'm about to come back with something equally as witty when a rumble, followed by a crack, comes from above us. At first I think it must be thunder, indicating a storm, but then the sound of claws clopping along the tiled roof make my arms prickle.

I stand and move to the front door, Aero mouthing *Careful* as I unhook the latch.

I take three deep breaths before throwing open the door, and then I crane my neck from left to right with enough force that I'm pretty sure I give myself whiplash.

As my eyes adjust to the pitch darkness outside, I find nothingness. Just a long expanse of dark.

I go outside to briefly have a look around before turning around and heading back toward the house.

"Maybe the wind?" I say, latching the door behind me.

When I get to the couch, Aero is onto his third cookie and has wrapped his shoulders in a cozy blanket.

"I'm sorry, but these cookies are ridiculous!" Aero says with a smile.

I smile back, taking a step toward him to give him a kiss, when an enormous crack and a blinding flash of green light send me hurtling to the floor. The front door behind me completely detaches from its hinges and cracks past my shoulder before shattering to pieces on the floor nearby.

When I look up, Aero is sat up in horror.

"Hi, darling, sorry I'm late," comes the ice-cold whisper of the Carling woman.

Forty

O ne moment, Felix is midair, catapulted by Gran. The next, he's sprawled on the floor.

My heart batters against my rib cage, and I feel like I could pass out. Nothing makes sense, like my world is spinning and crumbling all at once.

"Gran…" I whisper.

I'm looking at her but can't fathom the facts of the last twenty-four hours. Nothing makes sense.

Felix slowly gets to his feet, clutching his side in pain. "Aero, get away from her."

"Temper, temper," Gran says. She lifts her hand and cracks her knuckles, sending Felix back down on all fours and writhing in pain.

"GRAN, STOP!" I scream, leaping from where I'm sitting and crouching next to Felix as he struggles to breathe.

"My ribs," Felix says as he gasps for air.

I place my palm on his rib cage and attempt to perform a heal spell, but I know it's weak. It should patch him up enough, but we need to get out of here.

Gran circles the room like a tiger circles its prey. "Now, now, my darling Aero. Let's not make this difficult. I've been ever so good to you all these years, haven't I?"

"Gran, all those people?" I say, my voice catching in my throat as I try to help Felix up.

Gran stares at me like a cat does a mouse, and I'm engulfed in terror. I can't believe this is the same person I thought I knew.

"Aero, must I spell it out for you?" Gran asks, her eyes glowing with every step she takes. "I truly thought you were brighter than that."

I look around the cottage for anything I can use to protect us, but it's useless. I feel like a trapped animal as she saunters toward us.

"This has been going on for quite some time," Gran says, rattling her nails along the mantel atop the fireplace. "Mirabelle was the first I set up. But I never in my wildest dreams imagined I'd get to meet her great-great-great-whatever-granddaughter and blame it all on her."

Felix looks up, and I feel fury vibrate through him.

"You're evil," Felix spits, clutching his side. "Nobody will believe you."

"Ahh, see, that's where you're wrong. Because once I've completed the youth spell on Aero here, I'll take yours for good measure too. From there, it's a very simple indoctrination spell, and then the whole town will take my word for it that it was your dear, sweet old Aggie behind it all."

I want to vomit, but I hold it in. I grab Felix's hand and stand with him. My body hums with anxiety as I look behind Gran to see our best shot at getting out of here, slowly edging both myself and Felix toward the door.

Felix squeezes my hand twice, and I take it as my cue.

We lunge toward the empty doorframe as a spark of electric-blue light narrowly misses us from the end of Gran's fingers.

I grab the frame of the door and throw us both through it, into the cold darkness outside. I don't bother looking behind me, instead gripping Felix's hand tighter as we make our way past the lighthouse, ducking behind the oak tree next to it to catch our breath.

"Shit," Felix says, clutching his side and grimacing.

"Are you OK?" I ask. I wipe my forehead and inhale deeply, filling my lungs with the cool air.

"I think so." Felix puts his hands on his knees. "We need to get to town to warn everybody."

I nod, trying to think, when an enormous force, like an industrial fan, swirls from above.

Before I can figure out what's happening, the ground around me shudders, and my eyes adjust to reveal Papaver sitting patiently, wings outstretched and her eyes glowing in the night.

Felix smiles, shaking his head. "You beautiful big beast!"

Felix leads me toward her.

"Quick," I say, looking everywhere for a sign of Gran.

"Here," Felix says, lifting me onto Papaver's back before jumping up himself and giving her scaly head a kiss.

"Thanks, Paps," he whispers, which makes me melt.

The wind howls as Felix gives Papaver a nudge, and we lift into the night sky, Papaver's big, scaly wings becoming almost translucent as the lighthouse beam catches them. We soar through the sky and land softly in the town square, Papaver's claws clopping along the cobblestones. A few patrons from the White Horse stand with their jaws dropped as Papaver breathes a trail of steam in the cold night air, and Felix and I dismount.

"You stay here," Felix says, rubbing her gently on her neck.

We head through the double doors of the White Horse and head straight to the bar, where a burly old man with a beard stands pouring a pint.

"Have you seen Aggie?" Felix asks, clutching his side and trying not to show how much pain he's in.

"Not since this mornin'!" the bartender says, handing the pint to a patron.

"I'll go check the shop," I say, turning to leave.

"No, I'll go," Felix says. "You start letting people know what's going on. I'm sure she'll be here soon."

"OK," I say, looking around at the somewhat packed bar. "Be careful."

Felix makes his way to the door, smiling back at me as I look around for someone I recognize.

Huddled in the corner reading a book on sea creatures sits Miss Meadow, cradling a mug of something warm and chewing on a piece of string from her fingerless gloves.

"Miss Meadow," I say as I reach her, trying to sound as normal as possible. "S-Something has... I need to talk to you about... Have you seen Aggie?"

I'm struggling to make sense, and I can't think clearly.

"Aero, you look half daft! What on earth's the matter?" Miss Meadow asks, slowly closing her book.

I take a breath and slow my breathing. "It's—"

Before I can say another word, the windows explode, sending shards of glass flying through the bar and people ducking underneath tables and covering their eyes.

I huddle with Miss Meadow underneath our table as the last of the glass lands around us.

"Bloody hell! That's some wind!" Miss Meadow says, completely oblivious.

"That wasn't wind," I say, helping her up. "It's Blythe."

Miss Meadow's eyes search mine, trying to figure out what I'm getting at.

"As in, your granny?" she says, her innocent singsong sounding more alarmed by the second.

I nod, turning to look at the empty window frames in case she's waiting to cause more damage.

"There's not enough time to explain," I say, helping a few other patrons off the floor and dusting flecks of glass from their clothes. "But it was Blythe all along. Everyone who went missing. Every…" I take a breath and feel the tears come. "It was her. I need you to tell the others and be ready to fight. She needs to be stopped."

Miss Meadow bites her lip before straightening up, clearly ready to kick some ass if she needs to.

"Don't worry about a thing. I'll rally the troops. You just look after yer-self!" she says, blinking twice and spinning into a cloud of thick, purple smoke, vanishing in a flash.

Forty-One

It's PITCH-BLACK INSIDE WHEN I get to the Silver Teacup, and the door is bolted shut.

Anxiety grips my throat as I peer through the dusty window, peeking inside to find nothing but blackness.

"Shit," I say to myself, looking up and down the street for signs of anyone I might know.

Thinking fast, I turn on my heels and head for home, my boots scraping along the cobblestones and my ribs burning with every step. Panic licks my heels, but I just run harder. I get to the corner near the florist and lean against the crumbling stone wall, clutching my side and looking up into the night sky.

This is bad. Really, really bad.

I breathe in slowly, and my mind drifts to Aero as guilt seeps through me like muddy water. I can't believe how hard it was to trust him. How hard I fought to believe he was a good person and that I had nothing to worry about. All this time, he was trying to show me how much he cared and how little I needed to stress or worry about his intentions, yet I still couldn't handle it.

I pull myself up onto the stone wall and let my feet dangle off the side. My entire body throbs with pain. I need this pause. I need to remind myself how close I was to ruining everything with Aero for the sake of my own insecurities. After all this, even after finding out it was Blythe all along, he still cares about me.

I give myself a shake to try to let go of the stale feeling that has settled in my gut, but I can't help it. Tears fill my eyes, and I clutch the wall, my fingertips turning white as I let it out. I let myself cry, though every sob makes my ribs feel like they're caving in.

When I've finally let it all out, I wipe my nose with the back of my hand and climb down from the wall, landing as gracefully as I can in my messy condition.

I make my way toward home again when a rustling from behind stops me mid-walk.

"I hear you could use some backup," comes a familiar voice in the darkness.

When I turn around, Tomkin is standing with a hand on his hip next to Demelza, Winifred, Miss Meadow, and Gran, who strides over and wraps me in the biggest hug I've had in a long time.

After I've been smothered with kisses and had hugs from the rest of them, Demelza leads the way toward town, and Gran whispers a hushed spell to me under her breath, mending my cracked ribs while rubbing my back tenderly.

When we get to the White Horse, Aero, Fern, and Charlie have assembled an array of fishermen, bar patrons, and locals who have begun barricading the windows. After a second to take everything in, I realize just how powerful it is when you can truly trust someone. When you can let go and know that they've got your back, and that everything will be fine if you've got them in your court.

"Hey," I say, breaking away from the group and giving him a kiss. "How are you holding up?"

"I'm, uh… Yeah," he says, looking down at his shoes.

I can tell his heart is broken, but he's holding it together better than I thought possible.

"We're going to get through this," I say, taking his hands in mine. "I promise. You've just gotta trust me."

At those words, he looks up at me, and for the first time all night, his eyes light up.

"I can do that," he says, giving my hand a squeeze.

When we turn around, the others have begun to Blythe-proof the White Horse.

Demelza and Miss Meadow help two fishermen by enchanting a pool table to block a bay window next to the entrance. Tomkin barks orders at a group of young sailors, who are running around trying to find sharp bits of broken furniture for protection, and Gran is clutching her teaspoon to her chest, her eyes looking every which way and her left boot bouncing nervously.

It's been about half an hour when the first deafening boom shakes the walls of the White Horse. The rusty chandelier in the center of the dining room sways like we're on a sinking ship, and Miss Meadow lets out a squeak before cupping her hand to her mouth.

Aero, Gran, and I stand side by side, Aero's hand in my right and Gran's hand in my left.

"Everyone," Gran says, focusing intently. "You have got to believe that we will beat this evil."

I look around at the ashen faces, the fear in everyone's eyes.

"You have to *trust* that we will win," I say, looking around and giving Aero a wink.

"Now, what we have to—"

A booming crack makes my eardrums hum, and for a moment, I think I've lost all hearing. The entire roof detaches, ripping off and hurtling into the night sky, as if we were in the eye of a hurricane.

When the dust and debris has finally settled, we all look up into the purple sky and see her.

Blythe sits atop her broom, her eyes flaming red with arms stretched up toward the night sky. A cloud of static circles her like fluorescent willow branches.

"For the love of Merlin," Miss Meadow says as Tomkin clutches onto her, stunned into silence.

I look across at Aero, who is trembling as tears stream down his cheeks.

The first blast doesn't register as Blythe dissolves a fisherman into a pile of green ash right next to Charlie.

"Shit!" he screams as Fern sends a purple cloud toward Blythe, which she dodges swiftly.

"Pathetic," Blythe sneers, her icy glare homing in on me and Aero as a creepy smile spreads across her face.

"Eeny, meeny, miny, moe," Blythe chants, pointing at each of us slowly.

Fern continues sending up charms that Blythe swats away like summer insects, and I watch as the static surrounding Blythe grows stronger.

"Gran, we need to do something," I say, Aero's hand in mine squeezing tighter.

Gran nods, sending up a plume of purple smoke before ushering me, Aero, Fern, and Charlie into an unexposed corner.

"WHAT DO WE DO?" Demelza screams from across the room.

Gran points her teaspoon up at Blythe, who sneers again, focusing her attention on Aero.

Fern and Charlie duck underneath a table as a chandelier detaches from the ceiling, sending splinters of glass flying.

"She won't stop," Aero says, almost to himself.

"We'll make her stop," I say, my heart beating in overdrive.

Aero looks at Blythe and then lets go of my hand. "I'm not letting all of you get hurt because of me."

Panic rolls through my veins as Aero runs, jumping across overturned tables and chairs and through the wreckage. Blythe watches him move, an amused look spreading across her wicked face.

"AERO, DON'T!" I scream, shoving a chair aside to chase after him, only to be stopped by Charlie, who holds me back.

"What are you doing?" I shout at Aero and Charlie.

Charlie lets go of me, letting me fumble across the upturned room as I trip over some cracked floorboards that are protruding up like crooked teeth.

"Let's finish this, shall we?" Blythe says, making her way slowly toward Aero, who is beginning to slow down.

I look back to Gran. She's still pointing her teaspoon up at Blythe, her eyes closed and her lips moving silently.

Miss Meadow, Demelza, and Tomkin are huddled next to a shattered window frame, Tomkin shaking his head in horror as Demelza and Miss Meadow send sparks of static in Blythe's direction.

"Aero, please!" I scream, clambering up and pushing furniture aside to get closer to him.

"What are you waiting for?" Aero screams up at Blythe, sweat pouring down his back.

At that, Blythe swivels on her broom, skidding to a stop midair and pointing directly at him, her face still and terrifying, the small trace of amusement long gone and replaced with pure fury.

A bolt of fiery smoke leaves Blythe's outstretched palm, then slams into Aero's chest. It throws him writhing through the air and he lands with a crack against an already mangled wall.

I push aside a broken piece of table, and just as I reach him, he glows with a green-blue aura and lifts into the air, Blythe never taking her eyes off him.

"NO!" I scream, looking to Gran and feeling myself go weak.

"*Praesidiopu!*" Gran screams, and a gold sliver of light unleashes from her outstretched teaspoon.

I fumble in my pocket for my own teaspoon, repeating the incantation and letting my own sliver of gold soar into the air directly into Blythe.

Aero flips and contorts in the air, his face full of terror as Fern, Charlie, Miss Meadow, Winifred, Demelza, and even Tomkin point at Blythe, screaming the same spell, never dropping focus.

Blythe is hit again and again with the shocks of light, her focus on Aero waning as she's knocked back and forth on her broom.

"Charlie! You're doing it!" Fern yells, her face alight with pride as a thin purple streak of light flashes from the end of his palm.

With a final flick of my wrist, I repeat the incantation, this time sending a pure silver bolt directly at Blythe, engulfing her in sparks. She fizzles to a pile of ash, and Aero drifts quietly to the floor.

For a few moments, the only noise comes from the wind whipping along the cracked edges where the roof used to be.

Gran is sitting on the floor, surveying the damage quietly to herself, while Fern, Charlie, and the rest of the gang clutch various pieces of furniture and wipe sweat from their brows while taking deep breaths.

I race to Aero, who's lying in a pile of smoldering wood, his eyes flickering in and out of consciousness as a faint smile creeps across his face.

"Did we win?" he asks, his voice a raspy croak.

I squeeze his hand gently.

"We did," I say, looking at the pile of ash nearby.

"How?"

I look across at Gran, her hair disheveled and dust covering the bridge of her nose. Fern and Charlie lean against each other, a faint smile in the corner of Charlie's mouth after harnessing his powers. Demelza, Miss Meadow, and Tomkin pick through the debris, muttering about the state of things, while Winifred sits next to a flaming table, gently stroking Captain's chin.

"With some pretty powerful witches," I say, looking back to Aero. "And by trusting that we could."

Forty-Two

THERE ISN'T ANYTHING QUITE LIKE the sounds of Dorset Harbor in the morning. The seagulls sing overhead as I make my way past the florist and down toward the turquoise sea.

The fishermen yell across the dock to one another as sailors moor their boats, eating chips out of newspaper and exhaling puffy clouds of smoke from rustic wooden pipes.

I take a deep breath in and look up at the cliffs, the waves below battering up against the rocks, carving out new patterns and shapes as mermaids swim below the surface.

The showdown at the White Horse was already three months ago, but the town is still taking its time getting back to normal. People are slowly starting to look less anxious, the lines in their foreheads easing and frowns beginning to soften.

Mum and Dad went berserk when they heard about it all, but strangely enough, it brought them closer together. I'm still not sure where that leaves things with their divorce, but they have slowed up on the throwing of verbal grenades. For that, I'm grateful.

For the time being, I'm still living with Gran. We've been

studying the Silver Grimoire most evenings with Fern, Charlie, and Aero usually joining us. I have to admit, Charlie's getting pretty good since that night at the White Horse. I don't think even he realized how he managed it that night, but I'm pleased to say that he's continually getting better.

I turn left at the dock and walk across the boardwalk, each step making the damp wood groan as crabs scuttle away, dropping between the cracks into the water below. The sun dazzles across the still water as I take a deep breath, enjoying the smell of seaweed and crisp air as clouds overhead block out the sun briefly.

I turn and head uphill, my legs starting to burn as I walk to the Crock Pot Café.

When I get inside, Isla spots me and waves, pointing to a corner booth and mouthing, *I'll be with you in a sec!*

I walk over to the booth and scoot in next to Aero, who gives me a gentle kiss and takes my hand in his.

"Hey," he says, handing me a menu like I don't already know I'm getting the giant stack of pancakes like I do most Saturday mornings.

"Cute," Fern says from behind us, climbing into the booth first, followed by Charlie, who's looking extremely pleased with himself.

"Look at you, all giddy!" I say, unable to hide the grin on my face as Charlie sits down and drums his fingers on the table. "What's going on?"

"Oh, you know," Charlie says, as though he doesn't have a clue. "The sun's shining, the birds are singing, I got accepted into Yalford College."

All three of us freeze simultaneously.

"WHAT?" Fern says, slapping him on the arm.

Yalford College is the premiere magic college for miles. We all got our acceptance letters two weeks ago and have been freaking out ever since about Charlie.

"This is *epic!*" Aero says, drumming his hands on the table. "I *knew* you'd get in!"

Charlie blushes, suddenly self-conscious as we all throw praise at him like confetti.

After we've finished our stacks of pancakes and downed enough coffee to wake the dead, we head outside and dawdle up toward the Silver Teacup.

Since that fateful night, Aero has been doing fairly well. We've spoken about it occasionally, but I've let him do most of the talking. I want him to know that I'm here when he needs me.

When we arrive at the Silver Teacup, Winifred is reaching for Captain, who has crawled atop the window ledge and is refusing to come down.

"Oooh, you little sh—Hello, troops!" she says, bundling us into a hug.

"Where's Gran?" I ask as Winifred leads us inside, Captain peering down at us as we pass.

"At home, love," Winifred says, turning the sign to CLOSED as we enter. "Ready for your potions lesson?"

"I think I'll leave you lot to it," I say, giving Aero a kiss on the cheek. "I'll catch up with you a bit later."

"Suit yourself," Winifred says, beckoning the others to the back of the shop.

I close the door to the shop gently and make my way up the hill, passing the White Horse, which has finally got a new roof. Burned patches of grass sprout around the front, and a few stray pieces of wreckage sit wedged at odd angles in the dirt, still yet to be cleaned up.

When I finally get home, I stare up at the big, cozy house, and a sense of calm washes over me. No matter what has happened so far, whenever I think of my gran, I know everything is going to be OK. I guess that's the magic of my parents and grandparents. They're my safe place. The one haven that won't let ever let me down.

I walk up the porch steps and open the big door with a creak.

Newt bounds down the stairs two at a time, crashing into me and licking at my hands like they're covered in peanut butter.

"Hey, you big dope," I say, rubbing behind his ears.

"Darling!" Gran says, shutting the Silver Grimoire from where she's sitting in the dining room and making her way over to me.

I wrap her in an enormous hug, her perfume making me smile.

"Busy?" I ask, nodding back to the Grimoire.

"Oh, you know. Just a bit of light reading," Gran says with a shrug.

We head into the living room together and sit on the plush sofa, Newt following us and curling up into a ball on the rug at our feet.

"So," I say, cuddling a pillow to my chest and leaning back into the softness of the sofa. "Now that we've saved Dorset Harbor, what do we do now?"

Gran smiles, patting my arm softly and leaning back into the sofa as well, her feet dangling over the edge.

"My special boy, there's only one thing to do," Gran says with a cheeky grin. "Let's have a cup of tea."

THE END

Acknowledgments

OK, I'M GOING TO SAY I love you to a few very important people, so bear with me.

First, I want to thank my mum, whose unwavering support is what keeps me believing there's good left in the world. I couldn't be more grateful for everything, and I love you more than I could ever begin to put into words.

Dad, you gave me your copy of *The Hobbit* when I was ten years old and showed me what books could do for the imagination. I love you to bits.

Max, you're sprinkled throughout this book in so many ways. Even though you're my younger brother, I look up to you so damn much. I love you, mate.

Next up, Nan Barb. Thank you for letting me dress up in your magnificent gowns and wear all your jewelry as a kid. I got to be myself from the get-go, and I can't tell you how much I love you.

Nan Diane and Granddad Neil, you both are throughout this book in so many ways. Thank you for the many custard creams, teas, and magical trips up to the attic. I love you both gazillions.

Poppy, I know you can't read because you've got terrible eyesight (and you're also a dog), but I'll read this out to you. I love you. With all my heart.

I'd also like to give an enormous thank you to Annie and the entire Interlude Press and Chicago Review Press team for being so patient, kind, and caring with this book. It's been a joy working with you.

To my agents at Marquee, thanks for absolutely everything.

To my incredible friends:

- Diego Garcia Luna, you are the greatest friend I've ever been lucky enough to have, a brother and one of the coolest people I know.
- Sarah Watson, hi. I love you. You're wonderful and spectacular. Never change. Thank you for existing in my universe.
- Sophie Metcalfe, we are one and the same. I adore you on a weird level. You're simply glorious. Let's rule the world.
- Hayley Thomson, you're my sister and I adore you.
- Tanja Edwards, I love you to bits. You're my sis. And I will be flower girl at your wedding.
- Sally Curlewis, you are simply spectacular, and I adore you. Thank you for everything, sis.
- Elisa Vitagliani, you're simply glorious. Thank you for the endless FaceTimes and giggles. I love you.

Thank you for keeping me sane during a global pandemic and a crumbling planet. I love you all a ridiculous amount.

To the wonderful Geena Davis, thank you for being the greatest friend and mentor. I love you oodles.

Bundles of love to Uncle Tony, Aunty Kate, Laila, Faye, Dillon, Aunty Debbie, Joe, Mollie, Alex, and Aunty Syan.

And to all the young readers who picked up this book, thank you so much for joining me on this weird, wacky, magical ride. I can't thank you enough.

About the Author

HARRY COOK IS AN AWARD-WINNING actor and writer. Some highlights of his career so far include starring opposite Academy Award winner Geena Davis in the acclaimed film *Accidents Happen*, working alongside Sam Neill and Bryan Brown in the TV series *Old School*, and winning the Best Supporting Actor award at the prestigious FilmOut San Diego Film Festival for his role in the feature film *Drown*. His debut memoir, *Pink Ink*, was published in September 2018 to rave reviews. His young adult novel *Fin & Rye & Fireflies*, released in August 2020, was the winner of the Scottish Teenage Book Prize in 2022. *Felix Silver, Teaspoons & Witches* is Harry's second young adult novel. He currently lives in Los Angeles with his English bulldog Poppy.

CONNECT WITH HARRY ONLINE

🐦 HarryCook
f HarryCook
📷 harryjcook